I0574598

ALSO BY THE AUTHOR

GOOD BOY
BELLA'S BOYS
THE DEATH LIST
THE GOD PROVIDES
SUMMERHOME
A PRAYER FROM THE DEAD
IMMORAL DILEMMAS
WE ARE 13
THE CURSE OF KATIE ELDER

COMING SOON

ALL I HAVE LEFT OF YOU IS BLOOD
WHIRLWIND
THE WITCH OF NOVEMBER
THE TELLING OF THE BEES

A PRAYER FROM THE DEAD

THOMAS R CLARK

ST ROOSTER BOOKS
ONEIDA, NY

A PRAYER FROM THE DEAD
© 2023

A PRAYER FROM THE DEAD
(AUTHOR'S PREFERRED EDITION / REVISED)
© 2025

PUBLISHED BY ST ROOSTER BOOKS

SECOND EDITION

COVER DESIGN BY THOMAS R CLARK
INTERIOR PLATE DESIGN BY THOMAS R CLARK
INTERIOR ART BY STEPHANIE MURR

For Mariska and Atticus,

the real Abigail and Gabriel,

&

Jonathan, aka the Templar

TABLE OF CONTENTS

✟GREETING✟

"*Óró, sé do bheatha bhaile,*
Óró, sé do bheatha bhaile,
Óró, sé do bheatha bhaile,
Anois ar theacht an tsamhraidh."

Refrain from traditional Irish rebellion song

"*As it was in the beginning, it is now, and ever shall be. World without end. In the name of the Father, the Son, and the Angel of Death. Amen*"

Christian Reformation Army Prayer

⚜1: ASSUMPTIONS⚜

In the recesses of the Great Eternities expanding throughout the multiverse, pockets of reality reflect on one another. An infinite series of dissimilarities, molded by chaos, exist in tenuous harmony. Here, there is no yesterday, nor is there a tomorrow. There is only an ever-present now, constant and forever.

From the nether realms of the dark matter and decay, Death flies on great wings. Each beat propels the entity, gliding over the Seas of Time to its destination. A swirling wormhole opens, it is an offramp in the ethereal highways taking the traveler to a specific place at a particular, and constant, moment.

Death observes with curious morbidity...

⚜

IN THE YEAR OF OUR LORD 2144... THEN!

The Lamb's Crux casts its shadow across Manhattan Island as storm clouds piss acid rain on the ghetto's residents. The precipitation pelts Jimmy O'Neill, the constable on patrol this night. He's a beat officer with fifteen years on the force, and at this moment, he's leaning against a lamp post on 5th Avenue, doing his job—enforcing the nightly curfew. O'Neill's soundtrack is the rain's rhythmic assault on the plastic of his all-weather gear and the surrounding concrete, brick, metal, and tarmac.

Tonight, his labor entails observing the heretical Catholics in one of their houses of worship scattered throughout the island's tenements. A former Irish-Catholic himself, Jimmy was picked for this duty for being well versed in their ways.

Across the street, the spires of Saint Patrick's Cathedral disappear into the cloudy night. Jimmy's eyes aren't as good as they used to be. His astigmatism creates halos around the lights on the street, and the Cathedral's illuminated stained-glass windows.

The visual effect leaves him unsettled, and makes his task uncomfortable at best. It also obscures a pair of shadows moving in the darkness. Had constable O'Neill maintained his focus on the Cathedral, he wouldn't have seen them.

But, as fate would have it this day, an anomaly occurs. A slapping sound breaks the droning rhythm of the rain, and catches his attention. He sees something bouncing down the steps of the Cathedral before it disappears into the darkness.

"What the—" Jimmy's words are cut short when something touches the toes of his boots. He looks down to see a rubber ball, a children's ball, resting at his feet, the rain bouncing off the non-porous surface.

A ball? At this time of night? Where did it come from? He ponders to himself. *The Church?*

An errant sneeze forces him to turn his head, exposing more than a ball to the constable. Though O'Neill professes to his Puritan supervisors he no longer believes in the faith's ideologies and its saints, he still maintains a bit of pity and empathy for those who do. But he still must enforce the law. He brings his flashlight up. Its beam cuts through the falling rain, exposing a pair of black cloaked figures.

"Stop where yer at, folks. Yer out breaking curfew, unless ya've got permission papers, I'm sorry, but I'm gonna hafta take ya in," he says.

"Jimmy? Jimmy O'Neill?" One of the figures, a man, speaks.

"Is that you, Father?"

"Yes, it's Father Flanagan."

"And who's that with ya?"

"It's me, Jimmy, Molly Brennan," the woman answers.

"Ya know ya can't be out at this time of night, Father. Is everything alright?"

"Yes, yes. Well, no. I'm escorting Ms. Brennan home. She came for confessional and, well, I regret we lost track of time. I'm sure you understand this, Jimmy."

"That I do Father, but all I will do is let you go back to the Cathedral. I'm afraid I can't let you continue on. I won't arrest ya on account of who ya are. Ms. Brennan can sleep in the rectory, can she not?"

"That she can, Officer O'Neill. Thank you for your assistance."

"It's my pleasure, have a pleasant night Fa-" Jimmy O'Neill never completes the sentence. The words dribble into garbled nonsense. Jimmy drops his flashlight and claws at his throat before collapsing onto the street. He sees two cloaked figures, cowled hoods obscuring their faces, standing behind him as he lay prone. The glint of steel blade twinkles off the street lamp. His eyes blink and flutter, before closing, as the warmth of life slowly leaves his body with the blood pouring out of the wound on his neck. It mixes with the rainwater, creating pink and crimson cocktail, before washing down the drain.

The last words Jimmy O'Neill hears are Father Flanagan shouting orders to Molly Brennan, "Go! Now! Run!" The din of the nearby gravtrain's rail track rattles away as she runs across the street into an adjacent alley.

Constable James Patrick O'Neill's soul leaves this earthly vessel...

☦

...Death stands before the spirit of Jimmy O'Neill, Its arms open wide, like the wings of a great bird, awaiting the last name on Its ledger.

Jimmy isn't afraid. He's relieved.

"In the name of the Father, the Son, and The Angel of Death." He says, before stepping into Death's final embrace.

"Go! Now! Run!" Father Flanagan orders Molly, "And you two, go away. Now!" He directs this at the black cloaked assassins standing across the street. No words or body language betray any acknowledgement of the orders. The pair simply step back in unison, out of the light, and disappear into the darkness.

The priest waits a few moments, then starts after Molly Brennan. He makes it halfway down the alleyway before stopping in his tracks.

"Lord no!" Father Flanagan shouts, his hands covering his gaping mouth. Molly Brennan lay on the cobblestones, her eyes wide open, staring at the void. "Not you! Molly! No!" His words turn to sobs. Father Flanagan drops to his knees in front the woman's prone body. The priest takes her hand, and by reflex alone, recites a prayer.

He never finishes it. The sound of footsteps echo through the alley, and Father Flanagan stops his prayer.

"Where was she going, father?" A voice says, its host hidden by the darkness of the alley.

"Who's there?"

"An officer of the State," the voice replies. A man steps out from the shadows of the alley. He is dressed in the armor of a Puritan Templar, and armed with a long, wicked sword.

He recognizes the Puritan Templar, Fenwick O'Shea, who now stands at the center of the alley, a weapon gripped tightly in his hand. It is his infamous smartsword, *Mourning*, a weapon of legend and precision. In the other, a small leather-bound Bible is strapped to the palm.

The sword's blade hums with energy. Attached to his left eye is an optical sensor. A red dot at its center mimics the movements of his right eye, afflicting anyone who meets his gaze with an unsettling, uncanny valley effect. It only adds to his intimidation factor.

Not that the Templar isn't a tall and imposing figure in his armor to begin with. He stands in the alley next Saint Patrick's Cathedral, and his stance blocks Father Flanagan's way.

"We've been tracking a pair of dangerous assassins, who've been terrorizing the city with their gruesome murders. The trail has led me here. I've come to purify this place of its evils, where Catholic heretics brew their nefarious plans. I am prepared to do so with all the might that God has granted me."

"You. You're their lap dog."

"Aye. Fenwick O'Shea at your service, Father... Flanagan is it?"

"What do you want? Why would you kill this woman?"

"You mean this traitor who harbors assassins? She was out after curfew and fled from me. The penalty for fleeing an officer of the State is death, is it not?"

"You're mad."

"No I'm quite within my faculties. As far as this business is concerned, you will tell me where her children are hiding. Or you, and likely the rest of your congregation, will join Goody Brennan in Hell, or wherever you heretics go when you die."

Father Flanagan slowly steps back and away from the Templar. He knows behind him, less than a fifty yards away, lies the sanctuary of Saint Patrick's. Without another word, the priest turns and runs; his vision focused on the exit from the alley and putting as much space as possible between him and the Puritan enforcer.

The priest makes it to the street before the Templar catches up with him. Father Flanagan doesn't see the Templar, sword raised, ready to strike the priest down in midstep.

A sudden coldness fills the air. Two figures emerge from the darkness, one with a longsword and the other with a longknife. For once, the Priest is happy they didn't listen to him.

The blow is blocked, as a blackened blur comes between the Templar and the priest. This doesn't bode well for the Puritan; he's not expecting any resistance.

His sword strikes another, the latter blocking a blow that would have separated Father Flanagan from his mortal coil. A shower of sparks erupts at the impact, illuminating the rain-soaked street.

"Feck off, Puritan pig," the shape says with an effeminate voice, "she was our mother."

"That's right, you heard her," another, more masculine, voice says, "eye for an eye, right?"

The Twins, and they've seen their mother murdered. Father Flanagan knows this will be violent. He continues his dash, unabated to the cathedral. From the safety of the Cathedral's steps, he watches as the twins and the Templar strike and counterstrike at one another.

The Twins go by many names. To the Puritan authorities, however, Gabriel and Abigail Brennan as is written on their birth certificates, are known by a far more sinister monicker.

"You're the Templar. We've heard of you," Abigail says.

"Yes. And your reputation precedes you as well. The Irish Catholic fraternal twins, Gabriel and Abigail, also known as the Black Deaths. How quaint.

And they've come to claim a Templar's life. I think not." The Puritan enforcer responds, his voice calm, his demeanor showing no distress. He pauses long enough for effect. "Oh my, I am blessed by the Lord God today." The Templar adds.

"And why do you think that," Abigail says.

"Yeah, just what sorta shite do they feed you feckers, to make you believe their mumbo jumbo?" Gabriel adds.

"Why, because I get to end you today."

"Is that so?" Abigail asks.

"Aye." The Templar answers, and swings his sword at his adversaries. They answer in kind, deflecting his strikes and following up with opportunities of their own.

The Priest sees the Templar brace himself, and Father Flanagan is certain the man knows he is facing skilled assassins who won't hesitate to use any means necessary to take him down.

"Your reign of terror is over," the Templar says, his voice cold and unyielding. "Surrender now, and face justice for your crimes against the state."

"How about we end you for killing our Mum?" Abigail taunts him with another threat.

Father Flanagan watches the Templar raise his smartsword and prepare to strike, but the twins are too quick for him. Gabriel and Abigail emerge from the shadows, their weapons glinting in the dim light.

Without a word, Gabriel charges forward, his longsword flashing through the air. Fenwick O'Shea sidesteps the attack and counters with a swift strike of his smartsword, but Gabriel is quick to parry.

They dart around him, one to either side, striking from both sides with deadly precision. The Templar swings his smartsword with all his might, but he doesn't land a single blow.

Impressive, the Priest keeps his opinion to himself.

Abigail circles around behind O'Shea, her longknife poised to strike. The Templar spins to face her, narrowly dodging her blade and launching a counterattack. The two clash in a flurry of steel, their weapons ringing out in the empty street.

Meanwhile, Gabriel continues to press his attack, his longsword whistling through the air with deadly intent. O'Shea fights back with all his skill and training, his smartsword flashing and sparking as it deflects Gabriel's blade.

The battle rages on, each second an eternity, each combatant pushing themselves to their limits. The rain pounds down harder, turning the cobblestone street into a slippery mess, making it difficult for the Templar to keep his footing.

Abigail glares at him from under the hood of her cloak, her eyes burning with a fierce intensity. She lands a precision blow to his optical implant with the pommel of her longknife. The red light fades away and the sword ceases to vibrate.

O'Shea stumbles and falls to one knee, his smartsword clattering to the ground. The twins close in, their weapons poised to strike.

The Templar raises his Bible in a last desperate attempt to ward off his attackers. The twins' swords and knives plunge through his armor and into his flesh. He falls forward, hitting the street face first.

The twins stand over the fallen Templar, their weapons dripping with his blood, and look out into the night. The rain, still pouring down, washes away the bloody evidence of their victory.

☥

Death does not claim this soul today. After Father Flanagan and his progeny have left the scene, the Templar, stirs. Wounded but far from being on the Reaper's ledger, he opens his eye and sees Death before him.

☥

He stares at the rain falling with one eye and reaches over to the pommel of his smartsword. He feels their connection resume.

RESERVE POWER ACTIVATED. OPTICAL SENSOR DAMAGED. SERVICE IMMEDIATELY.

"Thank you. Set destination for home."

HOME?

"Yes, home. Now I know the truth."

THE TRUTH?

"That all of this," he points to the Bible as he unstraps it from his hand, "is bullshite."

FAITH IS A MANUFACTURED CONSTRUCT

"No shite," Fenwick O'Shea, beaten and bloodied, says to his smartsword. And tosses his Bible into the alley's gutter before dragging himself, and any evidence, away to his gravcar...

⚶2: ALL HALLOWS EVE⚶

On this day, a decade after the events we have seen, or NOW as Death perceives time and reality. Death chose to be transcendent, to evolve, and it does so on the heels of man's best friend. Innocuous, this small, white hound barks and bays in the darkness of a city's ghetto, becoming part of the soundtrack of the night.

It awaits the living instruments of its being, a pair of human siblings skilled in the clandestine aspects of war. They strike death with a sense of Deja Vu. It ponders for a moment, then remembers. A name stands out on the ledger.

⚶

IN THE YEAR OF OUR LORD 2154... NOW!

Deep in the multiplex maze making up the Eastern sprawl of New York City's boroughs, a crack of thunder shakes the earth. At the epicenter of the explosion, bolts of lightning rise from the ground and turn the night into day. A pair of gravbikes, running dark with their headlights off, turn a corner onto Sixth Street, four blocks away from the explosion.

A single rider sits upon each. They are pushing their vehicles to the extreme of the machines' capabilities. The riders' long black cloaks flutter in the backdraft as the bikes leave a crackle of ozone in their wake.

The shockwave from the blast catches both bikes from behind. Invisible hands flip the machines, catapulting the riders into the darkness. The riders pull their cloaks tight and tuck as they land. Inertia expends its energy as they roll to a stop.

The pair's gravbikes succumb to chaos. The machines tumble through the air. One rockets straight up, out of sight into the night sky. The other careens into a warehouse wall across the street and explodes.

The whistle of incoming ordinance heralds doom for where the pair sit. The smaller of the two riders jumps to attention and pulls their partner away from the impact zone. The duo falls onto the sidewalk, the force of their momentum carries the pair behind the stoop of a tenement brownstone.

Behind them, the street erupts as the errant bike succumbs to gravity and slams into the road. Cobblestones, metal and plastic blow out, creating a murder cloud of shrapnel. The stairs give the pair some measure of cover from the blast.

"You saved my life, didn't you?" Gabriel Brennan asks his sister, Abigail, as bits of sand and rubble fall on them. She nods, affirming his assumption, "for feck's sake, you're going to be unbearable to be around, now."

"Who, me?" Abigail smiles as the smoke and dust settle.

"Yes, you," Gabriel answers.

"I guess *you* can call *me* Saint Abigail, patron protector of twin brothers."

"Oh, please! Here," Gabriel stands up, bits of rubble fall to the ground. He offers his sister a hand, which she takes, and he helps her to her feet.

"Thanks. For the record, we didn't set the timer for long enough. I told you we should set it longer, maybe we wouldn't have been caught in the shockwave," Abigail says. Gabriel pretends to ignore her, until she adds, "I didn't have to save you," with a wink. Abigail blows her brother a kiss. He pretends to catch it.

"Craic. See what I mean? Un-fecking-bearable. You're really going to pull an '*I told you so*' here? Now? We stole the bikes from the barracks, they needed to be destroyed anyhow. They prolly had geotrackers on them."

"I'm your twin, it's what I do," Abigail replies, smiling.

"I'm older than you by a minute." Gabriel reminds her.

"And I outrank you, corporal," his sister counters.

"And now yer pulling rank, sergeant Brennan?" Gabriel's smile grows. This banter between the siblings is nothing new. They've perfected it over twenty-five years.

"Why not? My point is, now we have to walk back to Saint Jo—" She stops talking and pulls her longknife from its sheath.

Something captures Abigail's attention.

Gabriel answers by drawing his longsword. He knows to trust his sister's instincts.

"What is it?" Gabriel asks Abigail.

"I thought I heard a Witchfinder," she replies, her lips frowning as her brow furrows.

"Did you?" Horror covers Gabriel's face.

"I don't know. Let's go." The pair disappears into the dark of night, hoping death doesn't follow.

It does.

☥

The lights of an Irish Catholic cathedral burn bright on an otherwise darkened Broadway. It is one of many cathedrals scattered throughout the districts of the ghetto. The cathedrals are beacons of hope for the oppressed. They are places of worship and holy sanctuaries to the oppressed congregations of Believers who struggle to exist under the oppression of the Puritan government.

Within the walls of this holy structure, mass takes place. The Brennan twins, Gabriel and Abigail, now bask in the sanctity of the Saints under the Lord's roof. Dressed as they are, covered in camouflaging techcloaks, they blend into the shadows of the cathedral. The siblings hold their rosaries, counting the beads as they recite the prayer of the Blessed Mother in atonement for their sins.

"Saint Michael watches over us, big brother," Abigail Brennan tells her brother.

"And Saint Christopher delivers us from the evil of the Puritans, little sister," Gabriel Brennan replies.

The pair follow up with a chorus of *"Amen"* as they cross themselves.

"Honor thy Father and Mother in God's army. Hail Mary, full of grace." It helps ease their consciences for the horrid things they must do in the name of the Lord. In doing so, the brother and sister made their late Mum proud.

"Blood is the price for freedom, but ye've gotta pay the tax to God," Molly Brennan would say. Mum made sure the kids remembered the confessional. *"God forgives and forgets, as long as you play by His rules,"* she'd remind them.

After satisfying the tithe for their acts of war, the duo kneels at a pew and prays together. Once the routine is complete, the twins wait to partake in the Eucharist. The day promises to be routine.

Until the Witchfinder arrives.

☥

Death observes. It does not waiver. As the Reaper, it assails and claims those to be culled. Today is no different.

☥

The biomechanical assassin drops in on the congregation of St. John The Divine during communion at Saturday night's mass. As Father Ryan places the wafer in Judy McGee's mouth, his head explodes. She gets more than a mouthful of his holy sacrament before the CyberDrone rips her spine out.

Such a grandiose entrance requires a proper follow-up number to continue the momentum. The biomechanical Puritan creation doesn't fail to deliver.

With a wave of its metallic arms, the statues of the Catholic Saints lining the walls converge on the pews, plowing through them at unbelievable rates of speed. The juggernauts crush anything, wooden or otherwise, in their path. Within minutes most of the congregation, except for a handful including Gabriel and Abigail, are strewn about in some manner of mangled dismemberment.

The CyberDrone's magnetic weapons twist bone and rip flesh. The attack paints the walls crimson. Then it turns its attention to the survivors, one by one.

Family by family.

It starts in the back rows, with the Presbyterian family sitting there. The thing seems to relish popping the skulls of the O'Connor family one at a time, like matches in a book. The Brennan twins take advantage of the opening and flee, jumping through the stained-glass of St. John's onto the cold, wet cobblestones of Broadway.

The Witchfinder follows.

Gabriel and Abigail Brennan run down the alley, the fear on their faces hidden by facemasks under the hoods of their black cloaks. The glow of the moon reflects off the steel and chrome of the Lamb's Crux, casting streaks of darkness across the cobblestones. The duo dashes in silent synchronicity through these shadows. The lithe and athletic pair disappear every few yards, their cloaks fluttering behind them. It does nothing for their confidence.

Witchfinders can see in the dark.

Not knowing how close the Puritan killing machine might be, they reach a nook in the wall of an apartment building and slip into it. Winded and needing a rest, the recess offers them temporary asylum. Drawing the cloaks around, their figures blend into the shadows. They pray to God for the nanotech in the fabric to work.

If it doesn't, the Witchfinder will let them know.

Tech failure means discovery. Discovery means the last learning experience the twins will ever have. Clutching their rosaries under the robes, the twins silently mouth the words in unison, reaching out to

Saint Michael himself, for protection from the Puritans' death machine.

"Gabe. Do you think—" Abigail whispers to her brother. He grasps her shoulder with a firm hand and shakes his head as she speaks.

No.

Abigail stops talking. The CyberDrone can hear a teardrop roll down a cheek. She shudders in fear, knowing her whispers may have revealed their location. Her heart races as her fight or flight impulses grow.

☦

Death is perceived as cold and lifeless. This is not the case. Death has empathy. It knows most of those it takes are ready for the Afterworld. And those who are not prepared? They, too, shall ascend.

☦

The biomechanical CyberDrone plows through a wall, crumbling the rock supporting the three-hundred-year-old structure. Boulders of cement and limestone roll onto the street. A taxi flies overhead, whooshing by at top speed, leaving a trail of ozone behind it. The Witchfinder's scanners fail to discover the number of occupants, so it shoots a pair of smart missiles off from two of its limbs. One chases after the cab; in case the targets make it to the hovercar. The other flies into the cathedral.

The biomachine stays in place for a few moments, until it hears an explosion three, maybe four blocks away. The missile in the church detonates as the CyberDrone walks away. The four-hundred-year-old structure crumbles in on itself, falling to the ground, and creating an impenetrable dust cloud.

Alarms sound off and dogs bark in response. The biomachine's optics scan the landscape, seeking heat signatures from the escapees. The surface of the cobblestones betrays a faint trail, fading with each passing moment. Two sets of footprints, running away.

The Witchfinder gives chase.

The Puritan State tolerates the existence of the Catholics and their Saints. Laws forbid carrying effigies of the Saints in public. To the Puritans, they represented idolatry, making the Catholics one step away from being Polytheists.

Hated as the Catholics may be, this attack wasn't about persecution, at least on parchment. Puritan Homeland Security knew the Cathedral of St. John the Divine harbored heretical terrorists from the CRA insurrectionists. It must be eliminated, for reasons not only of heresy, but for sedition and treason.

The CyberDrone lurks down the alley as the last of the heat signatures fade away. A murder of crows flies off from their perches on balconies, leaving a small heat signature on the ground.

The CyberDrone's magnetic pulse cannons whir as they charge.

☥3: SOULS DAY☥

Death's omens come in many shapes. To some an avian, typically black, is a notion of things to come. To others, the presence of a feline signifies Death's imminent arrival. In some mythological beliefs, a white canine is the reaper's herald.

☥

Years of training has taught the twins Witchfinders, albeit terrifying to encounter, lack invincibility. Clumsy and unable to deal with intimate contact, the biomachines become vulnerable if you get close to them. You could disable them, cripple them, and get the hell away. Removing the thing's head did the trick. The biomachine could still operate after you chopped it off, but it couldn't see you or hear you. So, they wait, ever silent in the cove, for the moment to strike.

Abigail sees the white hound scurry out from behind a dumpster, terrified. Canine eyes make contact with the human girl. She sees the Witchfinder's long shadow looming, stretching out and down the alleyway. The faint umbra of a pulse cannon grows out of the darkness, the weapon now pointed at the mutt. She holds fast, knowing her instincts want to protect the dog, but she can't.

The animal runs down the alley. The Witchfinder chases after it in pursuit, each step clanging off the cobblestones and shooting sparks from the points of impact. The biomachine's momentum carries it past the alcove, and the twins watch in silence as it lumbers by. Then it stops, leaving its legs in a combat stance, securing itself to fire a pulse cannon.

Further down the alley, the dog stops and turns, staring down the biomachine, growling. The weapon churns and whirrs as bolts of electricity surround its length. It shifts back to discharge its load of high voltage death.

The hound growls in defiance.

The right arm containing the pulse cannon falls to the ground without firing. Metal bangs off rock, echoing down the alley walls. The CyberDrone's head spins one hundred and eighty degrees around. Its optical sensors reveal the culprit.

Behind it stands a defiant Gabriel Brennan, longsword in hand, frocked in his long black cloak and leather jumpsuit. A trail of smoke still lingers between the blade of his longsword and the stump of wires. Moldered flesh dumps green coolant out of the wound.

The secondary pulse cannon in the left limb comes to life. Before it charges, another blow, this from the front, disables the weapon. A long, jagged furrow grows out of the arm. Electrical arcs shoot with misfiring hydraulics spitting more coolant into the air. The thing's head spins back around.

Abigail smiles at her handiwork. Her longknife, nearly a sword as big as a gladius, did substantial damage. The blade twinkles in the moonlight. She flips her middle finger at the biomachine. Her brother stands on the other side of the CyberDrone. Their green eyes meet, opening a lane of silent communication between the siblings, premeditating a killing blow.

"Feck you!" Abigail shouts for effect and throws her longknife at the Witchfinder's optical cones, the horns of the helmet. The blade soars. Abigail can visualize its tip sinking into its quarry.

The blade misses.

The head unit twists, and she watches in terror as the knife sails past its intended target. Abigail hears her blade bounce off concrete and metal. The grim reality of her predicament sets in. Behind her, the hound lets loose a mournful, lamenting cry.

Gabriel swings his longsword at the CyberDrone's head hoping to finish the job and save his sister. The creature activates its glider wings. The polycarbonate panels pop out, blocking Gabriel's blow. The sword strike reflects off the wing, twisting the blade and Gabriel's wrist, sending it flying out of his grip. It skitters across the street, out of reach.

The hound bays.

A high-pitched tone, growing in intensity without any indication of a peak ceiling. Gabriel knows what this means. So does Abigail. Gabriel jumps onto the Witchfinder's back, grabbing hold of its glider wings. He draws a projectile pistol and fires. The bullets bounce off the CyberDrone's armor and energy field around the biomachine's sonic cannon.

Fundamentally a pulsating, spinning crystal capable of creating high-frequency soundwaves, the device rises between the unit's optical cones after activating. The object of its attention at this moment happens to be Abigail Brennan. The weapon fires and a pulse of sonic energy blows Gabriel off, tumbling to the ground.

Abigail dives away from the biomachine and runs for the cover of the dumpster across the alley. She hears the telltale shriek of the hypersonic gun and rolls. It doesn't save her. She doesn't make it halfway to the giant garbage receptacle.

Gabriel crashes into the cobblestones, raises his head, and watches in horror as the hypersonic burst strikes his sister. The weapon's discharge, forged from entropy and ambivalence, strikes the woman in the back. The sonic waves course through her in a millisecond, warping, and distorting the cellular matter within her body.

⚲

Time stops as she quivers in place. Abigail feels the weight of the Rosary on her breast and prays to Saint Peter for absolution. Then she sees the white hound watching from afar. Abigail hears its baneful howl rise over the whine of the CyberDrone's sonic cannon and marvels at how much it sounds like her brother. She finds it soothing.

The white hound approaches her, and licks her face. Abigail reaches to pet the dog. An ethereal arm breaks free of her corporeal form, and her ghostly hand scratches the hound's head. The animal turns and urges her to follow.

Stepping out of her physical form, Abigail chases after the hound. It leads her back to the dumpster where the hound jumps into her arms. It resumes howling, and Abigail joins in. Her cry is a keening wail, with their voices melding into one.

The chorus raises in pitch until it becomes a harmony with the sonic cannon. She watches the ghostly dog flicker and shift with her own astral being as her thoughts become disparate.

The shriek fades and is replaced by an ambient hum, the collective biological chatter of a world. Abigail finally understands and surrenders to her fate, becoming one with Death itself.

Death ascends, absorbing Abigail's soul within its being. The result blends the woman's essence and the infinity of eternity into one. Death, ever omnipresent throughout time and space, has reached an awareness unheard of.

With a new grasp of her perceptions, Abigail sees everything to ever be, and all that ever was. Her visions swim, swirling into an ether vortex, going back to the beginning of time itself, when darkness overcame the cosmos. At first there is nothing. Then a soundless flash of light and nothing materializes into something, leading to EVERYTHING. Rock and ice, darkness and light, life and Death, an infinite series *of chain reactions shaping all that has ever been and all that will ever be.*

Time catches up...

◈

...and Abigail Brennan bursts from the inside out.

"No!" Gabriel screams, stretching the vowel out into a howling wail. Broadcasting at a frequency higher than God created, the hypersonic blast perforates the cells of organic material in its path and disperses them. In layman's terms, the weapon turns anything it strikes into a splatter of protoplasmic goo.

A wet splatter erupts from what used to be Abigail Brennan. The blast of organic material paints the brick facade of an apartment building's back entrance in varying shades of pink, crimson, and black.

Possessed by grief, Gabriel pounces on his longsword. With his foot, he rolls the blade's tip over one of the round street stones, kicking the pommel up. He secures it and proceeds to go berserk on the CyberDrone. His first blow cuts off one of the glider wings. The second sinks deep into the biomachine's left leg, hobbling it. Gravity now works with Gabriel, forcing the Witchfinder to drop to a knee.

With its remaining free short-arm, the biomachine grabs hold of Gabriel by the waist. He drives the longsword's tip into the elbow joint and twists the blade. The metal snaps and shatters the tempered steel blade of Gabriel's sword, but the arm pops out of the socket. The calipers release Gabriel and dangle useless from the CyberDrone's side, held on by the organic material housing the thing's wiring and frame.

"Rot in Hell, you son of a bitch!" Gabriel declares. A battle fury the Irish heroes of old would envy drives his blows. He hacks and chops at the automaton with what remains of his sword, sending bits and pieces of it flying about, bathed in sparks. Then he hears the whine of the hypersonic gun come back to life and sees the turreted head spin on its axis.

Gabriel knows his time to say goodbye has arrived. He knows in this instance. Time, too, slows for him as it did for his sister moments before. Soon, he and Abigail will be reunited in the House of the Lord. He releases his useless weapon, allowing it to tumble in slow motion from his hand to the street. It clatters onto the cobblestones.

Behind the CyberDrone, Gabriel can see the white hound, the beast watches the carnage unfold before it. A lamenting cry fills the alley as time adjusts itself. A cloud of darkness spreads over the alleyway, blotting out the moon. Gabriel awaits the void of death.

☥4: HALLOWMAS☥

Death *as the Reaper is represented as a hooded skeleton wielding a bone scythe. With a swipe of the blade, it culls the herds of the doomed.*

At this moment, under the cowl is not a skull, but Abigail Brennan's pale visage. Death's invisible hands wield her scythe, a mortal construct connected to her by birth and blood. This instrument is far more valuable to Death at this juncture in time and space as a tool of culling. And thus, Death spares it from the ledger.

For now.

☥

Something yanks the Witchfinder up into the sky, throwing the aim of its hypersonic blast off. The sonic beam misses Gabriel and tears a divot through the masonry of a wall behind him.

The CyberDrone disappears, leaving behind the distinct ozone of a hovertruck in the air. The Puritan's called in a CyberMed for their precious automated demon. The twins messed it up, and it'd be tied up for a bit, getting repairs. Still, Gabriel needed to go, he couldn't pussyfoot around here in the alley. Sooner than later, more Witchfinders would follow.

He pulls the longknife from the wall and stares at what remains of his sister, a gory splat resembling strawberry and grape jam. Nothing recognizable. Gabriel doesn't want to be here. He casts his head down, and before he closes his eyes, a flicker of light grabs his attention.

On the ground, still intact, Gabriel sees Abigail's Rosary beads. He picks them up. A thin coating of pink mucus covers the beads, making them slippery in his grasp.

He fights the rising tears as he mouths last rites over the hamburger and sauce remains of his twin. As he holds her Rosary, the crows return to their stoops in the alley. The white hound dog runs down the cobblestones, toward Fifth Avenue.

Gabriel Brennan follows the hound.

Cloaked in black, clutching Abigail's longknife close to his chest, a morose Gabriel Brennan creeps through the shadows of Grand Street. The crisp, cold air of the November night steams his breath, leaving behind a dissipating contrail of fog as he moves. This indicator of his presence doesn't linger long enough to attract attention. The sulking man wishes to avoid contact with any passersby.

Each step Gabriel takes down the cobblestone street marks a curse on the wretched Puritan State. Every beat of his heart fuels the fires of hate brewing within his being. He holds back from lashing out, to do so would expose him. The emotions need release, and thus he wept. He closes his eyes to prevent the tears from burning them. A slideshow of memories floods his thoughts.

Flash!

Gabriel and Abigail, pre-teens dressed in frocking, standing at the altar before Father Ryan at their First Communion.

Flash!

Gabriel and Abigail, a pair of teenagers smiling with their prom dates in Catholic School uniforms.

Flash!

Gabriel and Abigail, graduating from Catholic School in their cap and gowns.

Flash!

Gabriel and Abigail, now young adults in olive green uniforms, at a Mohawk boot camp learning how to kill Puritans.

Flash!

Abigail saves Gabriel's life from a falling gravbike.

Flash!

Gabriel watches Abigail explode.

A chorus of thunderous roars erupt in his head. Gabriel opens his eyes, wipes the tears and snot away, then continues on his path.

Ahead, the white hound dog waddles down the street in the urban ghetto of Manhattan Island. Broad in the chest and short in stature, the dog's coat glows in the moonlight, giving it a spectral appearance. He doesn't intentionally follow the canine guide. The hound blazes the path of least resistance, leading Gabriel through the murky darkness of night.

Gabriel looks over his shoulder, a reaction of habit whenever he goes out at night. His eyes seek the familiar form of his twin sister. She always followed his point, watching his back, so he felt obliged to reciprocate. His heart jumps and skips a beat when a shadow moves.

Abigail?

No. It can't be Abigail.

Abigail is dead and I couldn't save her. The fecking Witchfinder turned her cells inside out and splattered them on the street ten minutes ago.

The anger resurfaces. He gazes at the longknife in his hand. The curve of the steel and crystal hybrid, the alloy flickers in the night's lights. The monofilament edge, whet by nanotech. The blade can cut water, slicing the molecules as it passes through, leaving a trail of steam in its wake.

Abigail's longknife. She called it Omega. The End.

He stops under the stoop of a closed market, pulls his arm back to strike the window. Then he freezes. He clenches his jaw and fist in unison and throws his hand to his forehead. He massages his skin with the gloved hand. He knows punching the window, or any noise will attract unwanted attention. The thing could be back, for all he knew it still hunted him.

Instead, he cries. The tears keep him company as he hugs the shadows. He needs to go underground. A side alley leads to a hidden manhole entrance, used by the CRA. He cracks a glow stick and drops in.

☦5: BAPTISM☦

Deep below the streets of Manhattan, cement-lined tunnels provide a secret, underground freeway for those not wishing to be seen above. Gabriel's familiarity in this labyrinth rivals many, with the exception of certain city DPW employees.

The sewers welcome Gabriel with the nose wrinkling stench of decay and methane. Groundwater seeps and drips through the walls, creating a humid environment. The light of Gabriel's glow stick reveals slimy, green lichen lining stress cracks in the concrete. He makes a mental note not to touch it.

Soon he finds himself nearing the train station. He marvels at the simplicity of using the city's sewers to infiltrate portions of the city. Three tunnels met at this point.

A whining whir fills the tunnels. Something mechanical slithers through the sewers, scraping against concrete and splashing water.

Gabriel sees a recess in the ceiling, leading to a manhole. Red lights illuminate the walls of the tunnel behind him. He throws the glow stick as far as he can down the sewer line and jumps up, disappearing into the recess. He doesn't wish to tangle with any more CyberDrones, at least for the time being. Whatever the thing might be down there, he doesn't know. A new model? A rat sniffer of some sort?

He watches as something chrome and sleek moves through the tunnel, tracking the source of light. The DPW's vermin killing AI CyberDrone fills the passage. It snakes past the intersection and stops. Three heads, lined with glowing red optical scanners, attached to extended necks, protrude from the front of the biomachine. Two bend and scan the tunnels to the left and right, the third turns its attention up the service entrance.

Hiding on ladder rungs, wrapped in his nightcloak, Gabriel grasps his Rosary and prays once again the nanocarbonites sewn into the fabric will trick the CyberDrone's scanners. Red lasers crisscross the interior of the shaft, climbing up its length. They trace the walls until the CyberDrone jerks its head back into the concrete.

The blow smashes a series of the drone's optical scanners, cutting the number of lasers in half and ending the scan.

The drone lurches forward and stutters in place, until it is dragged back by an unknown force. A battle in a tug of war with an invisible assailant begins. A rumble resonates and dust fills the tunnels after the main pipe collapses.

The security CyberDrone bursts free of whatever holds it and scurries down the tunnel to the left. Gabriel sees sparks and jagged pieces of metal where portions of the robot's tail once existed.

Gabriel ponders what would tangle with one to begin with. Might it be the elusive sewer crocodile? He doesn't sit around to discover what wrecked a Puritan CyberDrone.

Instead, he climbs farther up the shaft to the top of the service pipe. Once there, Gabriel latches himself to the iron rungs with a carabiner clip. He pulls Omega out of its sheath, and waits, holding the handle of the longknife in one hand and his Rosary in the other.

In the name of the Father, the Son.

A burst of green fire floods the tunnels below him. The flames created a vacuum, sucking the air out of Gabriel's lungs. Nausea overcomes him and he loses his breath. His eyelids flutter, his consciousness falls away. Vertigo takes over, separating time and reality.

And Holy fecking Ghost.

A whoosh of fresh air filled the void.

"Christ on a broken fecking crutch." Gabriel curses under his breath, and climbs back up the ladder.

He reaches the top and pushes aside the manhole cover. Climbing up onto the street, Gabriel can't believe what he sees.

The white dog.

The hound wobbles down the steps of a subway entrance and disappears into the shadows. Gabriel follows, as he did when seeing the hound earlier. He slides down the rails, jumping over the turnstiles, and hops on the first fastrain out of Manhattan. He doesn't care where it goes, he needs speed and anonymity, two things the fastrain provides. He wraps his nightcloak around him and sleeps.

☥ 6: SOLEMNITY ☥

The fastrain takes Gabriel Brennan out of Manhattan, into Brooklyn. His GPS beeps. The alarm warns him of the imminent approach of his destination. Gabriel sees the service garage's neon lights flickering ahead in the darkness. In the loft, he can see the gravtruck and its familiar paint job. The wrecker the Witchfinder called in for a last second save.

Gabriel unslings one of the four single-shot pipe guns he brought with him and primes the charges. Homemade shotguns made from plumbing supplies; they each held a single shot of shrapnel. Anything organic in the immediate blast radius would cease to live. They also happened to be quite effective at taking out delicate tech on Puritan CyberDrones.

Like Witchfinders.

He slings the projectile weapons. Abigail's longknife finds a home in a new sheath, hanging from Gabriel's belt, waiting to avenge its former mistress.

Gabriel works his way around the building, looking for a way in. Behind the parking garage attached to one side of the structure, a loading dock and back entrance door sit next to each other. The locked door doesn't remain locked for long. Gabriel jimmies it open. Before he closes the door behind him, he sees movement out of the corner of his eye.

It couldn't be, could it? He wonders. Then he focuses on it and realizes something remarkable stands in the lot.

The white hound.

The same white hound he followed the day before. He knew omens were for pagans, but this? This happened too often to be a coincidence. Could it be the same dog following him? He discards the notion it might be some Puritan robot dog they developed. Gabriel shrugs his shoulders; he doesn't have time to feck around with a creepy dog. He closes the door and locks it behind him.

Once inside the garage, it doesn't take long for him to find the Witchfinder. The battered biomachine resembles a fallen angel of death encased in a suit of medieval armor. Off the factory line, it comes complete with a historically inaccurate horned helmet, four weaponized arms, and retractable glider wings. Brand new, the biomachine is a sight to see. At this moment it resembles a partially dissected science project.

Within the automaton's steel and plastic shell, an array of circuit boards, wiring, and hydraulics controlling movement and weapons systems sit inert. Without the commands of the unit's AI giving its direction, a newborn baby is more of a threat.

"God bless Sunday," Gabriel says and blows the machine a kiss.

So far, the biomechanic replaced both of the CyberDrone's pulse cannons. The armor casing chassis, removed to repair the wiring and mechanisms Gabriel's longsword cut when he stabbed it, remained exposed. This couldn't be more perfect. Gabriel reaches into his cloak, retrieving a transponder attached to an ample mound of plastique explosives. He stuffs the bomb into the machine, away from servos or hydraulic stems.

He reaches into his pants pocket and pulls out a small transmitter. He feels around inside and places it on the underside of the armor's shoulder guard. Like his GPS, the tracker works off the satellites of the nearest space-faring nations to the Puritan States of America.

Surprise, you sons of bitches.

Gabriel stares at the machine, satisfied with his work. When the Witchfinder returns to its base, the explosive will activate, and.

Boom.

His smile left his face. A stain, a smear, catches his attention. Dried organic matter covers the offside of the machine. The mechanic didn't clean the hull, he may not have noticed the gelatinous, semi-translucent resin.

Abigail.

The stuff covering this like mud is what remains of my sister.

The grim reality of the previous night resurfaces. He slaps the side of the Witchfinder with his open palm in frustration. It dislodged a bit of the armor. The piece drops to the concrete floor with a loud clang. Free of any ambient noises, the clamor echoes through the building. Gabriel freezes in place, his face squinching as the sound seems to carry on through the shop. The piece of metal rocks back and forth, rattling and making more noise until the momentum gravity provided subsides. Gabriel breathes a sigh of relief.

Chaos breaks loose.

Alarms go off in spades, resonating throughout the structure. Bright, flashing lights fill the garage.

Sirens blare. Floodlights fill the building with bright, white light.

"Shite!" Gabriel says and punches the disabled Witchfinder's shoulder. Another piece of armor drops, adding to the sensory chaos. He hops down from the machine's torso, onto the chromed skid plate stationed beneath. The steel slaps the concrete as he lands.

Gabriel dashes through the building, running for the exit. He reaches the loading dock and the backdoor. He unslings one of the pipeguns and kicks the door out. An empty parking lot greets Gabriel. His heart pumps and he runs alongside the building, hoping nothing watches, hoping the police are still in transit. Brooklyn Puritan authorities tended to shoot first and answer questions in a hearing later.

Gabriel hears sirens in the distance. Moments later, the flickering of red and white lights creates a strobe effect on the street. He looks up and sees a fleet of gravcars moving at top speed in the direction of the mecharage. He won't have time to run far. He needs to hide and pray to Saint Michael. He doesn't wait to do the latter.

In the distance, a crack of lightning lights the ever-present skyline of the New York Ghetto. A second later, the thunder follows. The fastrain station provides at once both a place to hide from the Puritan law and shelter from the storm.

The hydraulic doors of a car swoosh open and Gabriel steps on board while he taps his smartwatch. The screen lights up under the cloak. He opens the activation app and turns on the timer as the train launches into motion.

The clock speeds down to zero and Gabriel falls into a seat and passes out from exhaustion.

Half a block away, the mecharage explodes. Gabriel does not hear it, but he sees it b build in the dreamscape forming in the clouds of his mind. The strength of the concussion blows the rain sideways, and the Puritan police to Hell.

Death claims her tithe.

In the physical world, the dozing Gabriel sits alone in a train seat. His body tosses and turns as his head thrashes. The dream world invades his muscles and nerves. Though unconscious, neither his mind nor body find rest. Instead, each is permeated with determination and vengeance to be fulfilled.

⚚

Gabriel flies, the fabric of his techcloak flutters in the sky. He is a voyeur, hovering high above the city streets. This vantage point provides him a clear view of the scene below.

A Witchfinder VI stands in a dark alley, battered and beaten. A pair of ebony cloaked figures surround the military-grade CyberDrone. They are ready to do battle with the manhunter.

One of them swings a longsword, cleaving into the armored hull. The other rolls and throws a longknife. The blade misses its mark, sticking into the wall. The hypersonic cannon vibrates and shrieks. The weapon discharges.

Time stops.

Gabriel plummets to the ground. An ethereal witness to his past, passing through his own body in the process. Waves of quantum protoplasm streak from the corporeal, following his astral form.

His sister hovers in limbo before him, their bright hazel eyes meet, glimmering in the shadows. Gabriel is shocked to see she has no fear in them.

"Abby?"

"*Hello, big brother.*"

"*How can I see you? Are you in Limbo?*"

"*Limbo?*" She laughs, "*oh, my poor naive big brother. You may be older than me by a minute and taller by a foot, but you're none the wiser. I haven't died, silly boy. How could we be talking right now if I were dead?*"

"*This is devilry. Yes, you did. I watched you die. Here, in this alley.*" Gabriel points a translucent arm at his sister.

"*There are no devils at play here. I'm alive,*" she beats her chest with a closed fist, "*See? I'm still alive, Gabe.*"

"*But I watched this Witchfind-*"

"*Be wary, Gabriel Michael. Remember the Word of God. A faithful witness does not lie, but a false witness breathes out lies. None who practices deceit shall live in My house, no one who utters lies shall continue before My eye-*"

"*Abby! Who is the liar?*"

"*Like a madman who throws firebrands, arrows, and death is the man who deceives his neighbor and says, 'I am only joking!'*"

"*For the love of God, Abigail! Stop quoting me scripture!*"

"They're all true, you know," she says, the words dancing from her lips, "and they're all lies. Everyone is right, and everyone is wrong."

"What do you mean? This madness doesn't make sense."

"It wouldn't be to someone trapped in the stream of reality. The truth is—"

A hound bays, the distorted wail obscures the words.

"What?"

"There is one God, dear brother, of this I am now certain. One God watching over all of us. And I have become one with God."

"What are you talking about? Of course, there's one God. But which one, Abby? Jesus? Allah? fecking Odin?" The howling from a chorus of hounds ascends into a cacophony of madness. The emerald glow of Abigail's eyes brightens until it engulfs the alley in a cleansing fire.

"Why it's Death, of course. I have ascended, becoming so much more than either of us could ever imagine, big brother. I am the Reaper, and you the scythe. I am one wi—"

Before he can process the words, Gabriel Brennan's astral body is jerked up, into the heavens. Helpless, he watches his sister shrink away, green *fire lapping across her body. It fills the alley, overflowing through the city and flooding the world. Time restarts.*

☦7: EUCHARIST☦

Gabriel wakes from his fretful nap as the train stops in Jersey, another nightmare in and of itself. He can't shake away the visions lingering in his mind.

What is going on? He asks himself. *The dream. It was so real. Abby?* Then he realizes where he is. *Jersey of all places! The land of diners. You can't turn left or worship as you please here. What a shit place.*

Of all the states to be on the run in, Jersey isn't the worst. Yes, Jersey Puritan authorities tend to shoot first and answer questions in a hearing later. But it could've been Massachusetts, the home of gallows and stakes. Like most people attached to living, Gabriel preferred not to have his neck stretched or his flesh burned for believing God canonized mortals.

He thanks God, slips onto the street, wraps Abigail's Rosary around his pistol, and pulls his cloak tight. Ice cold drops of rain inch their way closer, building into a crescendo as dark storm clouds blot out the moon. Across He watches the lights of the Puritan civil authorities' racing through the air to their mystery emergency.

Motherfeck—

Fifty thousand volts of electricity flood over his cloak. His body tenses and spasms, sending him into a seizure. A second blast of electricity courses through his body. He drops to the ground. The cold rain beats down on his body.

"In the name of the Puritan States of America! Don't move!" A soldier covered with an olive-green poncho shouts. Gabriel sees him standing in a defensive stance, aiming a shockrifle. He resembles a fisherman on a wharf with a harpoon gun. Instead of fish, this man caught other prey.

He taps the side of his radiophone. "Alpha Base, this is Sergeant Edler on patrol. I got one of them, male, early twenties, he matches the description of the suspect in New York. I took him down with the SHOCKer. I repeat, I have one of the CRA terrorists. Send a riotwagon to my coordinates to pick up the trash."

"Roger that, Edler. Be careful, they're dangerous." The dispatcher replies.

"I've got this one, don't you worry."

Gabriel knows if he can reach a weapon he can silence the fool, but he can't move. The double dose of electric blasts tensed his muscles into paralysis.

"You ain't so smart, buddy. I watched you come out of the train and run down here. You're a CRA heretic piece of shit, I think I'm going to whoop your ass on principle alone." He kicks Gabriel in the side.

Something, a blur at first, catches his eye. Standing across the street, the white hound watches.

Are you shitting me? Gabriel asks himself, questioning if he ever saw a real dog. *How is this thing popping up everywhere I go?*

It sits, and it watches. The dog's presence now became more than incidental. The hound howls. The soldier hears it and shakes, his skin white with fear.

A brilliant light fills the night. Gabriel and Sgt. Edler watch a radiant ball of green fire streak from the sky. It crashes into an empty lot half a block away.

The strength of the concussion blows the rain sideways and strikes Sgt. Edler in the back, sending him to the ground. He loses his grip on the gun. It skips across the parking lot and into the street. Gabriel rolls with the blast as the spasms subside.

The din of the falling rain takes over, interspersed with flashes of lightning and cracks of thunder. Everything else remains quiet. The whine of a riotwagon breaks the stillness. He sees the multi-colored emergency lights turn from white to red as it closes in on their location. Gabriel pushes himself up and withdraws a grenade.

"May the Saints preserve ya!" the freedom fighter says, giving a truncated version of the last rites. "As it was in the beginning, it is now, and ever shall be. World without end. Amen," he pulls the pin, drops the explosive, and dives behind the concrete wall of the garage.

The hound bays.

Sgt. Edler, a faithful Puritan soul, will never wake up. The grenade roars smoke, fire, and shrapnel at the soldier. The bits of hot metal pierce the man's bones and flesh. When the smoke clears, what remains of Sgt. Edler resembles a chunky pudding, ready to be stuffed into a sausage casing.

Gabriel runs up the stairs to the top of the parking garage. Once there, he pulls out his pistols, checks their ammo, and holds one in each hand, pointing them in the direction of the oncoming riotwagon. The Army vehicle is filled with a team of Puritan zealots, all of them wanting a piece of the CRA terrorist. He'd give them scraps to fight over.

The riotwagon, a modified hovervan, reaches the parking garage, hovering at eye level with the roof. Gabriel fires both pistols, aiming at the vehicle's underside. The bullets tear apart the delicate gravpads keeping the car aloft. It plummets twenty-five feet to the ground and bursts into flames, the fire dancing off the armored car's metal frame. The falling rain sizzles off the immolated vehicle, creating a dense, steamy fog in the parking lot. Gabriel smiles.

Maybe I'll get out of this alive after all.

The euphoria over his success evaporates as a hypersonic blast shoots out of the cloud. The bolt of energy strikes a portion of the parking garage's top floor. The sonic blast from a Witchfinder's headpiece-cannon rips through six inches of steel and crumbles granite. It does all of these things to a four-square foot section of the building. Rock, concrete, and metal turn into an anti-personnel explosive, transforming the rain into mud.

Gabriel runs for the cover of the stairs and jumps down the flights, skipping the steps from landing to landing. Each time his feet hit concrete and tile, his self-confidence in surviving an encounter with a second Witchfinder in so many days diminishes. By the time he reaches the bottom, he's accepted the notion of imminent death.

He pauses to look out the glass of the double-doors from the stairwell of the parking garage to the adjacent parking lot and survey the situation. The steamy fog dissipated; however, sheets of rain continue to come down in buckets, making visibility difficult at best. Gabriel can make out a pile of twisted metal and shattered glass, the remains of the riotwagon. On top of the wreckage stands a RiotCon CyberDrone.

The smaller crowd control Witchfinder provides Gabriel with a microsecond of humor. Though he dubs it Witchfinder Junior, he doesn't underestimate the simpler AI run model. The biomachine lacks the missile batteries and secondary arms of a field model. Although it possesses a hypersonic cannon, the magnetic pulse cannons are replaced by SHOCKer lightninguns.

Gabriel draws out his sister's longknife, kicks the door open, and charges at the biomachine.

It shares a personality flaw with its big brother. Witchfinder Junior doesn't care for conversations with close-talkers. Omega's monofilament edge cuts through the raindrops as he runs. A ghostly trail of steam grows behind him as the longknife separates the hydrogen molecules. The reaction marks his path, stretching from the garage door toward the CyberDrone.

The rain stops and Gabriel can hear the biomachine charge its hypersonic cannon, preparing to deal with an incoming threat. Gabriel plans to be more than a threat before he joins his sister. He reaches the killing machine in record time to make any professional athlete envious.

The Witchfinder spins its helmet turret around and fires the hypersonic cannon, but not at Gabriel. He watches the blast shoot up and disappear into the clouds. Something huge falls from above and blots out the distant lights of the New York skyline and the Lamb's Crux. The sonic cannon fires into the sky, again.

Gabriel feels his ears pop when the weapon is discharged. He grits his teeth from the pain. Gabriel strikes with Omega. He runs the longknife across the backs of the CyberDrone's bent knees. The attack would have hamstrung or crippled a human.

The Witchfinder doesn't fare much better. Its armor offers no protection from the knife's subatomic edge. It slices through ballistic nylon and steel, separating flesh from metal and plastic. In the process, the crystal and steel alloy blade cut the unit's main hydraulservos in one of its legs. Gabriel smiles.

Taking down Witchfinders is becoming my specialty, he muses.

The bipedal, cyber-organic tank swings its arms around on a freewheel. One grabs Gabriel from behind with a clawed hand. The steel fingers squeeze into his shoulder, sending a jolt of pain down his arm. He drops Omega. The knife sticks into the concrete.

Gabriel pulls out an enormous revolver with a large scope attached to the barrel. He pulls the firing hammer back with his off-hand palm as he draws the weapon back. Despite the caliber of the weapon, he knows the handgun's ammunition will be useless against the biomachine's armor. Exposed servos and other parts impossible to cover, on the other hand? Well, they prove to be more effective targets.

Gabriel aims the pistol at the CyberDrone's wrist and squeezes the trigger. The fifty-caliber lead and steel jacketed bullet rockets down the handgun's rifled barrel, spinning as the superheated gasses propelled it forward. Fire blesses the exit with a crack and the retort echoes off the parking garage.

The bullet strikes the rotator cuff controlling the arm holding him. The armor-piercing round nearly sheers the appendage off at the joint, but it holds fast. The servo-unit grinds gears, yet the arm is stuck in place.

With a hobbled leg, the CyberDrone lists to one side, preventing it from aiming its hypersonic cannon at Gabriel. The soldier aims his revolver at the rotator. He steadies his firing arm with his off-hand, and—

An ear-piercing shriek fills the night.

The Witchfinder Junior stands upright with a violent jerk. Gabriel's shot misses the mark and reflects off an armored plate. The biomachine's arm still holds Gabriel's shoulder. He wiggles and twists, but can't escape its grip. He reaches down to grab Omega. The handle of his sister's longknife remains a few frustrating inches out of reach.

The hypersonic cannon fires again at the mystery target Gabriel can't see. Something the CyberDrone's sensors can sense and perceive as a threat. The creature fears it enough to shoot random blasts at it, hoping to hit something.

Gabriel manages to pull Omega out of the ground by locking his foot under the knife's pommel guard. His fingertips tickle the polished silver pommel. If he can pull it up another inch with his foot, he'll be in business. Gabriel pulls up with his leg as he bends down, and snags the longknife's hilt. He wants to relish this significant triumph. Time won't allow it.

A pitch-black void envelops the head of the Witchfinder Junior. It pulls the CyberDrone off the ground. The creature's bad leg dangles underneath it next to Gabriel, who now hangs helplessly from the crippled mechanical appendage. The biomachine continues to rise off the ground. Gabriel swings up at the arm with the longknife. Omega strikes true and separates the cybernetic wrist from the rest of the limb.

Another shrill cry wails, and the hound howls in answer.

Gabriel falls and time slows as he tumbles toward the ground, a dozen meters away. He watches the Witchfinder fall up from him and disappear bit by bit into a vast void. He sees the white hound, still sitting across the street, baying as if its existence depended on it. His body and this void move further and further apart until Gabriel hits the ground and time returns to normal.

The impact shatters the concrete underneath him. Gabriel can't move. He can only watch the darkness devour the Witchfinder.

The sound of ripping metal tears through the night. Moments later, Gabriel watches awestruck as two separate halves of the Witchfinder Junior, now useless chunks of burned flesh and scrap metal, fall to the parking lot. Wires pop and sizzle, hydraulics hiss from each clump. The stink of burning meat fills the air. Gabriel turns his head and stares at the wreckage for a moment, and then he looks up.

Hovering above him in the sky, a great beast covered in black down screeches and roars in victory. Held aloft by a beating pair of feathered wings, the monster isn't quite a bird or any species Gabriel knew to be a stowaway on Noah's Ark. Gabriel notices the rain didn't stop. The beast's wings, capturing great pockets of air, deflect the weather away from its proximity.

The creature radiates magnificence. Thick hind legs with wicked, taloned feet balance the thin forelimbs, stretching out to hold the incredible wings. The long, robust neck ends in a horn crowned head where spiky growths of bone poke out of the slicked back plumage. Each of its emerald green eyes glows, lighting a halo around the creature's head.

A massive crocodilian, snout lined with rows of twisted, snaggle toothed fangs sits where a beak should be. A long, slender tail with a fluke of thick feathers assists it in navigating the air. The beast lets out another belief defying shriek, pulls its massive wings in, and dove toward the earth, The monster's eyes leaving streaks of ethereal green in the slipstream behind it.

A dragon? A motherfecking dragon? How in the feck can this be a dragon? It's 1973! They don't exist! Gabriel ponders this paradox as the beast closes in. Would it breathe fire down upon him, incinerating him? He clenches his sister's Rosary and prays. Not to Saint Michael, but to his new saint, before closing his eyes, and letting oblivion caress him.

Saint Abigail. She of the eternal wonders, beatified in His amazing grace, guardian of the righteous and enlightened.

The heavens answer their ward with a banshee's cry, and carry Gabriel Brennan home.

☩8: DUTY☩

Transcendent, Death observes all that has or will happen simultaneously. Time is not linear, and neither is Death. Like Death, time simply IS. Death is everywhere, and nowhere, all at once.

☩

Far from the sprawl of New York City, in the vast northern wilderness of New York State, a dozen Puritan border rangers stand before the stoop of a cabin in a wooded valley, hidden in the northern mountains.

Stone and rough-hewn pine boards, gray with age and sealed together with pitch greet them. The structure's porch faces the east, welcoming the morning sun at their backs. A pair of windows flanks a thick, oak door- its surface pocked by carvings and sigils men of God fear. The sun glares off the glass in duplicate, giving each window the appearance of having pupils. Smoke wisps from its stone chimney, coloring the glen with the aroma of burning pine and sage.

The soldiers approach with caution. They traveled far, questing to find the valley and the cabin within on a mission of utmost importance. Hidden from the technology of men in the northern borderlands, the cabin is isolated from most forms of communication outside of the tried-and-true courier.

A single man wearing a scarlet jacket, marking him as an officer in the Puritan army, emerges from the group and walks up the steps. He stops at the top, his hesitance at what he must do showing. Finally, the officer knocks. There are a few moments of unease as they wait. Then the door opens, and the men bow their heads.

The hooded figure standing before them is tall and gaunt. The soldiers gasp in unison. A gloved hand flips back the hood, exposing the disfigured face of a man who once resembled Christ Himself. A jagged scar cuts across his left eye and much of the flesh is replaced by a metal optical housing. In place of the eyeball, a cybernetic implant moves in tandem with his left eye.

Behind him, resting on pegs, the courier can see the glistening blade of a crysteel smartsword. Its name is Mourning, and the man's renown for proficiency with this weapon creates fear in those who find themselves opposed to him. These soldiers possess no fear of the weapon. They are but messengers.

"Good day, Sir," The officer says, his voice shaking.

"You knocked?" the tall man replies.

"Yes, sir-" The fear of him steals the courier's voice, making him unable to complete his sentence.

"Look at me, for the love of God," the man interrupts, "All of you. Despite rumors to the contrary, I'm not going to hack you to bits with my sword." The men look back up, and though they appear to be terrified, the tall man knows something else scares them more. Why else would they be here? "Well, what is it? I know you didn't make an impossible journey, only to stand there and stare at me." he coaxes the courier on.

"In the name of the Father, Son, and Holy Ghost," the officer whispers, and makes the sign of the cross with the cupped and pinched fingers of his right hand, "Forgive me, Lord. I parlay with the Devil." The tall man rolls his eye.

"Devil?" He snorts, "No more than you, gentle sir, I am but a humble servant of the Lord God and our savior Jesus Christ," he raises a scarred eyebrow, "I'm certain you didn't come all this way to make accusations on my integrity, Sir. I didn't catch your name?"

"Barrett, Colonel William Barrett of His Lord's Border Rangers," he reveals.

"Well, colonel, what is it? I haven't got all day," the tall man lies.

"I was told to bring you this from the Reverend President himself." He reaches into his coat and retrieves a rolled bit of parchment. He hands it to the tall man, and steps back, again turning his head to the ground. His command follows suit.

The tall man unrolls the scroll and reads its words aloud.

"November 2, 2174

To Master of the Puritan Templar Order (retired) Fenwick O'Shea,

It is with great urgency that I send you this correspondence. The activities of the heretics in

Manhattan's ghetto have forced the hand of the Deacons in Parliament. Dire times require drastic measures.

God has a need for your skills, once again, Sr. O'Shea, otherwise we would not have gone through the trouble of sending couriers with this message. Your proximity lends to the speedy resolution of the matter.

Our heretic informant in Manhattan has been unwilling to continue with our agreement and needs persuasion. We are aware of your history with the criminals known as The Black Deaths. We are of the opinion you would like this opportunity to resolve past issues with the respected parties.

After your duty is fulfilled in this matter, we promise to not call on you again, no matter how dire the circumstances.

Your servant under God,
His Most Honorable High Reverend,
President of the Puritan States of America,
Jacques Perlicious"

The tall man listens to each word as he speaks them. The syllables roll off his tongue until they drift to silence. Chirping birds and the buzzing of insects grow to a clicking crescendo and abruptly stop. The chill of a winter breeze grows in their stead.

"Thank you, colonel. That will be all." The tall man says, breaking the silence. He turns his back to the messengers, and closes the door to the cabin.

✠

"Well, my love," the man known as Fenwick O'Shea says to no one in the room, "I think we should ready the mechmount for travel. We have one last bit of work to do in the name of our Lord God." On the mantle, the sword's blade pulses in a hue of crimson.

WHAT IS IT?

"Revenge."

AMEN, only O'Shea can hear the smartsword's answers.

✠

Somewhere in the northern borderlands of New York and the Mohawk Nation, a small herd of great ungulates moves into a snow-covered meadow to graze on the grasses sticking through the snowpack. They stand two to three meters in height, covered with matted ruddy hair. The males carry gigantic racks of antlers on their massive heads. The winds pick up from the north, brushing the exposed grasses like waves and fanning the long hair of the creatures. One of the herd trumpets and the rest stop in their tracks. Something is amiss.

Above the valley, a small cloud bank resembling a storm forms, and is moving to the south and east on the wind. Arcs of lightning trace out from the smoky cloud, bouncing to and from its black, brain shaped mass. It seems an anomaly, a single storm cell with a mind of its own.

The lead bull swings his head, snorting. He appears agitated and stomps the ground with his massive hoofed feet. The booming echoes, the rest of the herd looks to him and take his lead as he turns from the meadow and trots around the herd. When he is satisfied all are present and accounted for, the bull sounds off again and the animals thunder off, away from the meadow, heading to the woodland hills.

Moments later, the cloud flies into the meadow. It is not exactly a cloud. Within its expanse is an unexpected anomaly. Wings extend from either side of a vehicle suspended in the air. Straddled upon it, his hands gripped on the mechmount's handlebars and eyes covered by goggles, is Fenwick O'Shea.

Bolts of electro-magnetic force emit from the tips of the wings, propelling it at high speed. The expended energy transforms into the cloud, leaving behind a signature contrail.

DNA ASSESSMENT LAUNCHED. MATCH FOUND.

"Where is he?"

SATELLITE TRIANGULATION COMMENCING. TARGET LOCATED WITHIN MANHATTAN GHETTO. WE PROPOSE DRAWING OUT THE PREY WITH A DECOY.

"I like this idea. Are we in coms range with the High Reverend's office?"

AFFIRMATIVE.

"Send this message. Inform the heretic. Let him know I'd like to set up a public meeting."

AND THE TITHE?

"The price is," he pauses for effect, "Biblical. Increase speed," O'Shea orders his smartsword's AI, "we have an insurance policy to claim."

AFFIRMATIVE, the AI responds. The cybernetic vehicle's head raises slightly as its thrusters come to life. A crack of ozone follows, and the Templar whizzes across the plain. A trail is blown in the snowpack, leaving a ditch in the center of the field.

As the mechmount and its pilot continue to become a speck on the horizon, the bull ungulate trumpets. Then, slowly, the herd returns to the field to finish their dinner.

⊕

After they've eaten their fill, the herd moves on. Soon after, a second black cloud stops over the snowy meadow and hovers eerily in place, seeding the ground below with a hard rain, melting the snow below. The air under the cloud shimmers and crackles, with static electricity arcing about from raindrop to raindrop, to the ground and back into the cloud itself. After a few moments this continues to increase into a frenzy of purple and white sparks until the spectacle finally explodes, a tower of burning ozone stretching from the ground up to the sky, blowing away the black cloud in a clap of thunder. Then there is nothing but acrid smoke on the ground wafting up and across the meadow; a steamy mist hovered over the ground.

Death, in the form of a naked woman, stands up from the smoke and fog. Ashes fall off her blackened, soot covered frame. She is lean with long hair, dripping in black liquid, her hands grasping shards of black obsidian. Death opens her eyes. They glow a bright red. She laughs, and a high, screeching banshee wail filled the valley.

Death knows what awaits the Templar, after all, she is everywhere.

☥9: HALLOWMAS☥

Icy winds from the west cause temperatures to plummet and snow to fall across the far northern wilderness. The full moon's lunar glow is bright and to its right, a red scar twinkles. Fall fights for a hold on the land, but the frozen grip of winter invades the night far too early in the season this year. With help from the assault of cold and lake effect snowflakes, high winds blow what remains of the leaves off the trees. The evergreens bend and sway in time to the wind, resistant to the attack. Snow falls and accumulates by the foot within a few hours.

Across the waters, scattered about their ranks, mingled painted sylvan warriors holding assault rifles wait for their backup to arrive. Adorned in modern body armor, accented with buckskins, bones, and dangling feathers, they blend into the woodland. Tensed up, like caged animals backed into a corner, they stand at the ready, awaiting the command to attack.

The snow comes, creating white-out conditions, obscuring them further. When the snow breaks, they watch a patrol of Puritan soldiers trapped and disoriented in the sudden blizzard conditions.

The evening sun sets behind the disparate army, reflecting off the river's glimmering surface. The waters bubble, creating a fog. The mists hide something rising from the depths. The twisted points of deer antlers break the surface first, followed by a head with a single, glowing red eye. It's a massive construct of metal and plastic. The Mohawks call their Self-Automated Battlemech 'The Wendigo.' It launches out of the water, flying across the sky.

And it's hungry for Puritan souls.

⊕

The sky wakes from its nocturnal slumber with a flash. Out from it bursts a crimson flare, hurtling to the earth from the heavens, whistling and burning through the sky. High above the valley a crack of thunder pierces the darkness in a black cloud moving to the south on the wind. Arcs of lightning trace out from the smoky ether, bouncing to and from its brain shaped mass. It seems an anomaly, a single storm cell with a mind of its own.

Falling past the full mid-winter moon, the object's path reflects off the snow-covered landscape. It draws a line across rolling hills dotted with patches of wooded groves, and through valleys surrounding frozen rivers and creeks. Within these throngs of trees, the eerie light brings the exposed foliage to life. Lunar shadows, falling from evergreens, battle in silence with the twisted skeletons of seasonal maples, ash and oaks, silhouetted in neon red.

The flare, arcing across the terrain, leaves a tendril of thick smoke hanging in the air behind the burning head. It strikes the earth with a dull, sizzling thud. Snow and ice melt on impact. It splashes down as much as it crashes into the earth. A mushroom cloud of debris grows out of it, with a tower of burning ozone stretching from the ground up to the sky, blowing away the black cloud in a clap of thunder. Then there is nothing but acrid smoke on the ground wafting up and across the meadow; a steamy mist hovering over the ground. The trail above, hanging in the sky, dissipates and everything is quiet, again.

A flurry of powder erupts, breaking the serenity. Barreling across the snowpack at full gait, a pack of wolves runs away from *something*. The scent is wrong. It isn't natural, it doesn't belong here. The scent turns foul and fetid. They don't dare bark, whine or howl, fearing whatever the *something* is will discover them. On instinct alone they run from the source. Their fear blinds their primitive minds, and they fail to see what stands before their path; a squad of humans making their way through the snowpack. In other circumstances, the wolves would run in a different direction. Fear, though, has a funny effect on those in its grasp. They blaze a path, and behind them, the wake of their galloping bodies jumping in and out of drifts, a crimson haze burns, urging them on.

Snow and ice drip from the trees and cover the swooping landscape up to a man's waist. But it doesn't stop Bloody Bill Barrett and his Bastards from following the wolves and running for their lives through it. Snowshoes aid the dozen Puritan border rangers in their plight, elevating the elite fighting men above the snowline as they put as much distance as possible between themselves and the Mohawks chasing them.

A seasoned tactician, Bloody Bill's reputation precedes him and the men under his command. Over the years of his command, Barrett's Bastards spilled more than their fair share of Mohawk blood and secured the Colonel's alliterate epithet. The rangers' despicable actions in battle earned them theirs. Together, the triumvirate of Bloody Bill's Bastards drove fear into the souls of God-fearing fighting men in the borderlands between the Mohawk and Puritan lands.

But this wasn't a military operation with him on the offensive. It was a returning courier mission he was ordered to oversee personally. They were not prepared or ready to confront these... *heathens*. And their machine.

The Mohawk's Wendigo battlemech didn't fear a Goddamned thing. The Wendigo darted through the woodland, harassing the rangers under Barrett's command. This breed of mechanical bogeyman harvested bodies, dead or alive, to feed its power cells, making it similar to the mythical tribal monster in at least one aspect.

Its weapon of choice turned out to be rocks. It threw rocks and stones, the weight of which no single man could bear, let alone throw any distance. The rocks fell from the sky, harassing Barrett's rangers, possibly herding them in some direction. The Colonel smelled a trap looming, and his years of experience in situations of this nature confirmed his notions. He couldn't let it herd them. Instead, his rangers would need to reach their outpost and make a stand.

Reaching the security of the blockhouse by nightfall would be their only option. Colonel Barrett's personal assessment of the situation amounted to utter bullshit and a single solution.

Dig in.

They entered a thick forest, and his first gamble paid off. The dense trees hampering the falling rocks and providing some cover. But more than anything, it gave them a moment to rest and gather their bearings. The Colonel raised a fist high in the air. The rangers behind mimicked the silent command, sending their commander's order down the line.

A single scout ran to Barrett's side, his assault rifle grasped in his hands. An icicle hung from the tip of the weapon's bayonet. He flicked it off before reporting. Flying rocks could be heard, cracking through the tree limbs. Both men looked up and around for falling debris as often as they made eye contact with one another.

"Sir."

"Sergeant Dodge," Bill whispered, "spread the line out, finding the outpost in this bloody white out is our number priority. Running isn't going to win this fight. We need to make them play this game by our rules, understand?"

"Aye, sir!" The Sergeant saluted and without another word, shuffled off on his snowshoes to pass the Colonel's instructions on. A bird whistle confirmed the execution of the orders and the rangers continued on through the trees and the rolling terrain. As the sun fell, the temperature dropped with it. The haze of the rangers' breath, freezing in the cold air, grew into a gray fog hovering above the ground. It made an already difficult situation worse.

Counting on God's good grace to once again be on his side, Barrett's optimism outweighed his fear. A hubris of this magnitude often led to the fall of men with relevant beliefs. The Colonel, however, lacked the arrogance of a narcissist. He genuinely cared about the lives under his command. So instead he weighed, then played, the odds as well as any successful gambler. Before long, the battered rangers found their commander's prayers working in their favor, once again.

Near the crest of a tall hill overlooking the surrounding river valley, the lights of their outpost came into sight.

✟

Tendrils of smoke rise from the lights within the outpost. As the rangers move closer, they understand why they lost radio contact. Soot covers the walls and timbers lay fallen within, protruding through the windows and ceiling. The former location of a door fell to the ground in whatever disaster befell their base of operations.

The rangers creep upon it with quiet grace on the snow. Barrett points two fingers at his eyes, then at his men, and finally at the interior of the outpost. Sgt Dodge and another man comply with the silent order without question. After setting aside their assault rifles, they draw long knives from their belts and scurry into the structure.

A few tense moments pass as they wait. In the distance, the crashing of rocks can be heard, again. The impact of their ordinance grows in volume, a clear sign the Wendigo gained ground on them. A sigh of relief can be heard when Sgt. Dodge pokes his head out of the opening and waves his hands, signaling the all-clear.

"Fall out!" The colonel orders, and the rangers make haste transferring from the field to the outpost, slinking in one at a time.

Barrett's Bastards, the border guard rangers in service to the Lord, came from all walks of life. Barrett himself grew up in the Irish Catholic ghetto, converted and joined the Puritan military. Take the Greco brothers, who immigrated from Sicily, Salvatore and Guisepe.

"You two, the Greeks," Barrett calls out the rangers. Short, stocky, and clean-shaven, the duo resemble a couple of Roman Legionnaires. They salute the Colonel, "as you were," the men relax some, "we need power. Find the backup generator and get it fired up." The brothers salute once more and go about finding the power supply.

Sgt. Dodge reports.

"Sir," he clicked his heels and saluted, "the building is clear, nobody's been here in a long, long time. It looks like they ransacked the place shortly after we left with the message for the Templar."

"Secure our power reserves and give us heat. Get someone on the satellite phone to get us reinforcements. Then, set up perimeter guards here, and here," Barrett points out spots to the left and right of the entrance, "we also want coverage on this flank, here," he points to the other end of the outpost. Sergeant Dodge and corporal Roberts salute the colonel and split up to follow through with his orders.

The rest of the rangers do their best to secure the entrance and other openings. With rocks and stones and other objects bouncing off the roof, they know they're in for a long night. Splinters, dust, ice, and snow sprinkle down on the rangers. The unrhythmic beat of the falling rocks adds to the men's uncomfortable situation, throwing their inner ears askew. Barrett finds himself a victim of vertigo moments before the Greeks spark up a raging fire.

This pleases the officer. Warming the bones of his men and lighting up the place will improve the rangers' morale and their desire to live. He cares about the men under his command. The men followed him with such a high degree of enthusiasm, one might think they valued him more than the silver paid for their services.

A large boulder slams into the wall, creating such a racket the men all duck for cover.

"That's it!" Barrett trumpets as he pulled his saber out, "I'm tired of pussyfooting around with these sons of bitches. Let them eat the Lord's lead, gentlemen!" He brandishes the sword over his head before swiping it down and giving the command to, "FIRE!"

The assault rifles come to life, turning the field into a death patch. Powder clouds fill the outpost and area surrounding the building.

"FIRE!" Barrett commanded a second time. More bullets fly.

"Hold!" The Colonel orders his men, Once again holding his saber high above his head. He looks at the amount of smoke filling the air. His plan carried an unexpected side effect. A wall of sulfurous fog now surrounded the outpost. It offered more cover and hid them from the enemy, "Cease fire! Conserve ammunition. Looks like we scared them off."

Barrett's assumption seems to be correct. Nothing more falls on the roof or slams into the walls. Until the wind blew, and the bravest among the rangers wept in dreadful fright.

☧10: EPIPHANY☧

Gabriel wakes from a dream wherein he flew. His entire body aches. He realizes he still holds his rosary in one hand, and his sister's longknife in the other. It takes him a minute to figure out where he is.

The last thing he recalls is falling away from the Witchfinder Junior.

And a Dragon?

Now? He is on the street. Somebody or something brought him back from Jersey. He doesn't know who. Or what. Gabriel sits up and hangs his legs off the curb. He cracks his neck, and stretches his arms, then stands and stretches his legs. He feels as if a truck ran him over. Then he remembers. He wastes no more time and moves into the shadows.

By the time the grieving man reaches Saint Patrick's Cathedral, many blocks later, the tears have dried. He waits for mass to end, and watches the white hound disappear into the shadows of the sanctuary's steps. When the congregation leaves for the evening, Gabriel goes to the back and sneaks in through the delivery entrance.

Once inside, Gabriel makes his way to the confessionals. He rings the bell and sits in shaded silence, the lights of the sanctuary bleeding through the screen of the confessional. He waits for Father Marcus Flanagan to come from the rectory and sit across from him on the other side of the screen. The young man shakes in anger and grief, wanting to deny the truth.

Abigail. Abby, his twin, his partner in this war against persecution.

Gone.

The priest enters the box, sits, and slides the screen open. Gabriel pulls his facemask down. The fabric, saturated by his tears, drips down his chest onto the floor and red velvet of the kneeler.

"This is late for a confession, my son. Who comes seeking the Blessed Virgin's forgiveness?"

"Thank you, Father Flanagan, it's me, Gabriel Brennan," he pauses, fighting back more tears, "Bless me, Father. I am not without sin," Gabriel says, fighting to keep his composure.

"We are born with sin, my child, it is through the blood of Jesus Christ and the Saints that we find forgiveness. What is your confession, my son named for the archangel of strength?"

"I am not strong, Father. by no will of my own. oh feck!" The priest coughs, unappreciative of Gabriel's choice in verbiage. "I'm sorry, Father. I'm so, so sorry."

"What is wrong Gabe?" Father Flanagan asks, his voice showing concern for the young man, "You never cuss in front of me."

"My sister—" he stops, choking on phlegm as he tries to speak the words, "Abby. My sister is dead, Father!" Each word he speaks rings out like a bolt of thunder. Within moments, Gabriel's world washes away in a great deluge as his tears return with an apocalyptic ferocity. He stabs the longknife into the confessional's wall. The blade sinks in, the tip reaching four inches into Father Flanagan's side of the box.

"*Abby! Abigail!*" Gabriel burst out in grief, crying his sister's name. Somewhere, outside of the church, a hound howls. The grieving twin tells Father Flanagan everything.

"We need to get you to a medic, Mr. Brennan," Father Flanagan says as he exits the confessional box. The priest looks back at the tip of Abigail's knife sticking through the wall and shakes his head. He opens Gabriel's side up. The younger man stares at him with a blank expression.

"What's a medic going to do? They can't bring my fecking sister back. I shouldn't have come here, Father, but I didn't know where else to go."

"You need treatment for the shock."

"Shock? I watched a Witchfinder turn my twin sister—a person I have spent almost every one of my waking hours with—into something the consistency of wet snot. I'm not in shock. I'm pissed. I want my sister back, you son of a bitch!"

"Gabriel! Please! We've got a *safespot* in the basement of the rectory. We can hide you there. Food, water, medicine. A bed. A prayer altar. You'll be all set until this blows over."

"Blows over, Father? This ain't gonna blow over. We fecked up one of their multimillion-dollar demon machines. The Puritans will go door to fecking door and tear every church apart until they find me, or somebody they think looks enough like me, to hoist up and burn at the fecking stake. And then they'll tithe our blood to pay for the damages. They give no shites. I told you they already blew up Saint John's and killed everyone inside. What do you think they'll do to this place?"

"How do they know it was you? Did you expose yourself to them?"

Gabriel pulls his mask up, yanks Abigail's longknife out of the confessional. He slides it through his belt and pulls his cloak tight.

"No. I didn't. But they have her DNA from the scene. That's all that's left of her Father. DNA. If I didn't make myself clear enough earlier."

"You're being irrational, Gabriel. Sit down, please. You're in shock."

"No. I gotta keep moving, get off the island. I can go hide with the Presbyterians. They at least do the Blessed Sacrament. Maybe I can book passage up to Europe and seek asylum, or disappear into the Mohawk lands."

"Presbyterians? Mohawks? You can't be serious, Gabriel. They won't take you in. They don't want problems. You're a religious freedom fighter and insurrectionist. You're a problem in their eyes."

"Great, I come to you because this is what we're told to do when shite goes south. And you are not helping one bit. What the feck do you propose I do?"

"You can start by watching your language, I've been patient with it until now. Go to the bunker, take a shower, drink some tea and rest," Father Flanagan places his hand on Gabriel's shoulder, "we'll take care of it. Now, go, do as I tell you. You're a soldier in the Lord's army, right?" Gabriel nods in affirmation, "then listen to one trusted with His Holy Sacrament. The Lord will take care of us. Go to sleep, Gabriel, please. I've got some phone calls to make."

Gabriel follows the priest to the bunker's secret entrance, hidden behind a bookshelf on a sliding track.

Ten minutes later, sleep overtakes him, but his subconscious mind remains wide awake.

Gabriel dreams, and the dreams bring chaos. The visions, shifting and swirling, lie to him. They tell him his sister lives. He knows this to be untrue. In between these lies, the event replayed over, and over in his head.

Abigail's longknife misses the mark.

The squealing shriek of the hypersonic cannon stops time.

Gabriel's strike is deflected. He makes eye contact with Abigail, betraying the inevitable. Her green, emerald eyes reflect his own, creating a primordial moment. Through them, he can see the infinity of the cosmos and the truth to all the mysteries of men.

Time's return is marked by a wet, farting sound.

He stares at what he can never unsee, burning the effigy in his mind. The vision fades to black before the lies begin anew. Denial transforms into reality, and the whole damn thing replays itself. Over, and over, through each breath of sleep.

☦ 11: BAPTISM ☦

Dawn comes, but in the forests surrounding the borderlands it is pitch black. Shadows cast by the rising sun are filtered through the trees. The leafless birch, oak and box maples create skeletal shadow puppets. The tall pines add to the darkness, and together the trees of the forest create a labyrinth. Fallen timber and brush litter the ground, and unless a traveler follows a well-trodden road, they can become disoriented and lost within its expanse. The wilds of the borderlands often rewarded its visitors with death from the elements, or worse.

Unless something life threatening sent you into the woods seeking refuge in its dark grasp.

The latter is all the motivation Privates Abraham Cooper and Colleen McCarthy need to cut their own meandering path through the sylvan maze. Their trailblazing is by choice, another aspect some might have thought foolhardy. But something drives the duo, a force they fear more than the danger of getting lost in the woods. It is their hope the evil pursuing them will, too, be at a disadvantage.

As it would be, neither of them are dressed for the weather. They are clad in the uniforms of Puritan regulars complete with assault rifles, with long bayonets affixed to the top. Their teeth chatter, a combination of being cold, the chill of the blowing winds, and terror.

The promise of sanctuary motivates their plight for survival. Whatever chases them wants more than their flesh. Abraham uses his rifle to cut the brush away. Still, twigs and branches beat on their bodies, scratching the exposed flesh on their hands and heads. As a result, lacerations and bruises decorate the pair's faces.

"I think the road to the outpost is just ahead!" Abraham says.

"Please, Lord God, let it be so, I don't know how much longer I can do this!" Colleen adds, her words exasperated by exhaustion.

"I'm almost certain." He swings the rifle's barrel about, continuing his attack on the brush and foliage with the blade of the bayonet. It is rather effective for the task. He grows more frantic in his strikes until he finds he swings at nothing.

The path ahead is a clear, grassy field. They both know this field borders the road to outpost and refuge. They hurry across the trail. Though muddy, it is preferred to the woods. Abraham looks over his shoulder, making sure their pursuer isn't seen. So far, luck is on their side.

A smoldering cloud rises from the remains of the outpost. It blends into the rain, joining a rancid stench of sulfur, wet charcoal and burned flesh sticking to the wind. A dozen dead bodies, bent and twisted, are indistinguishable from the broken timbers of wood.

Colleen McCarthy screams.

"They're all dead. Billy, oh my God Billy! All of them. A dozen rangers. Gone. Oh, no. The Colonel!"

In the center of the wreckage is a single body, crucified on an X of boards. It is Col. William Barrett. She stares, unable to move forward from the shock. Instead, she shakes and rubs her arms with her hands, over her jacket, desperate to create friction and heat. She twitches as her arms move up and down. The desired effect isn't working in the deluge.

"The fecking savages. They did this. We should be dead, too."

"If this was the Mohawks, that means—" They twist and turn their heads, looking for the source of the sounds they hear in the growing light of dawn.

And pray it's nothing evil.

⚚

The sound of a mechmount walking breaks the unnatural silence surrounding the scene of carnage. The giant black cybernetic beast, covered in crimson red trappings, trots into view on the road. A cloaked and hooded rider sits upon the beast's large back. Standing a good twenty hands high, the mammoth cyberhorse's thick, metal legs cut through the wind with ease.

"Sir!" Abraham waves his rifle in the air, hailing the rider. "It's not safe here! The Mohawks!"

Rider and mount stride up to the man, woman, and ruins. The mechmount bows before the duo and the rider dismounts. He places a hand on the pommel of a sheathed sword, attached to his back. A large red cross is embroidered into the left breast of his tunic.

"Mercy, governor! Mercy. We survived this massacre by being away from the outpost." Abraham manages to say. The man grunts. He withdraws the sword. The crysteel infused blade pulsates in red and crimson, the cold air sizzling along its curved length.

"And yet you remain here?" He asks.

"We have no place else to go." Abraham replies.

"Mourning says otherwise."

"Morning? I do not understand."

"Mourning says you were supposed to be here when the *skraelings* came."

"*Skraelings*? We don't understand what you are talking about. Good sir, please. It's evening, please, we don't understand why you say it's morning."

"It's time for Mourning of the dead. May the Lord preserve you, fools." He replies. The cloaked man brings the sword up and swings it down. The pair gaze in horror as the armed man completes the arc, neatly cutting Abraham and Colleen in twain. The strike is quick, giving neither victim an opportunity to scream.

First their arms fall to the ground, cut off at the elbows. Their assault rifles drop in pieces, alongside their extremities. Then their torsos slide off from their bodies at the waist. There is no blood. The heat the crysteel blade radiates cauterizes the wounds. This traps the blood supply in the upper half of their bodies, keeping them alive until the shock and trauma of being bisected shuts down. Without diaphragms, they can't scream, and thus Privates Cooper and McCarthy gurgle unintelligible gibberish as they join their dead friends.

⚕

Mourning, Fenwick O'Shea's crysteel smartsword doesn't stop pulsating. The Puritan Templar enforcer, known to some as simply as the Templar and to others as the last person they would ever see, shrugs his shoulders in dramatic jest.

THREAT ASSESSMENT HIGH, the sword continues to tell him through their connection.

"Oops. I was wrong? Wasn't the first time. Won't be the last. Sorry about that," He salutes the bodies of the slain survivors, tapping his forehead with a finger. The sword's vibration increases and glows like a hot iron.

THREAT ALERT! THREAT ALERT! THREAT ALERT!

His mind guides his senses, *Where in the name of God is the threat?* He thinks as he assesses the area.

O'Shea finds his attention turned to the ruins. Something shifts in the pile. Broken pieces of timber shake and rise up. Pieces of timber and stone, lubricated by the mud and muck of dust slide off a matchstick golem—in fact, a gigantic battle automech—rising from the rubble.

Attached to the center of its head is the crucified body of the outpost commander. To the left and right sides of the 'X', the automaton's optical sensors glowed red and orange.

"Jesus, Mary and Joseph! What is this?" O'Shea says.

WENDIGO BATTLEMECH DETECTED. WARNING. WARNING. THREAT ASSESSMENT HIGH, the sword tells him. A giant fist of steel slams into the earth only inches away from where Fenwick stands. It shakes the ground, but not the Templar.

He casually flicks Mourning around with a twist of his wrist. The subatomic edge of the crysteel blade slices through the steel and fiberglass wrist unabated. The mech's fist crumbles into a pile of wreckage at O'Shea's feet. The robot jumps back, a high-pitched wail screams from the severed servos.

To O'Shea it sounds like the machine is shrieking in agony. *It feels pain?* Fenwick grins. *This is going to get interesting.*

The smartsword moves of its own volition, striking the construct at critical points on its frame. The legs give way to the weight they can no longer support and the mech tumbles into itself. The unit's head, still masked with the crucified commander, sits atop the rubble. The dead man's flesh pulses and oozes with moisture, droplets of a foul-smelling liquid trail off the body, leaving spiderweb strings behind them. Fenwick feels Mourning pull him to the body.

"You see this?" He asks the smartsword

THREAT ASSESSMENT. THREAT TERMINATION IMMINENT. DISABLE MICRO-INTELLIGENCE MODULE, the sword replies.

"There you are, you bastard." The Templar says as Mourning slices the dead man in twain. The flesh peels apart as the blade cuts across from the man's groin, through his sternum until it bisects the head. A crimson glow grows in intensity as the sword opens the body up, worms and tendrils writhed about the man's innards.

O'Shea punches the skull with his off hand and twists it inside the cavity, mortaring the brain matter for a minute as he searches for something. He stops, smirks and raises an eyebrow, then withdraws his hand. Grasped in the Templar's fist is the mech's control AI.

"Got you." He says, examining the shard before casting it to the ground and striking it with Mourning. It shatters and disintegrates. He slides the weapon into its scabbard and climbs back atop his mechmount.

"Did you like that?"

YES.

"Good. Alert Puritan authorities. Tell them I've secured and destroyed the tech threat from the

Mohawks. I regret the outpost was destroyed and a new garrison must be implemented STAT."

AFFIRMATIVE. MESSAGE SENT; WE HAVE RECEIVED AN ENCRYPTED MESSAGE FROM THE HERETIC.

"And what does it say?"

THE HERETIC HAS OUR INFORMATION AND HAS SCHEDULED A MEET FOR EXCHANGE.

"Reply, tell him to bring the tithe to seal the agreement."

MESSAGE SENT. THIS HERETIC WILL GIVE US WHAT WE WANT?

"Yes. The secrets of the Black Deaths."

THIS PLEASES US.

"As I knew it would."

Thunder cracks, a second later lightning illuminates the gloom, and high winds blow in the rain. Huge droplets slap the Templar and his mechmount. He kicked his spurs into the ribs of the cyberbeast and it rears up, kicking its forelegs in the air, before they disappear into a cloud of snow, moving south.

☦12: CONVENT ☦

Death's scope is as vast as the known universe. As it transforms and absorbs, it cannot ignore its duties. Far from the city's concrete jungle, a far more natural forest welcomes Death in all of its glorious majesty. Outside the wilderness, a place of God is built, a fortification protecting the Believers living within its walls from the dangers of the Borderlands.

Death ponders. If all the world is the Lord's House, then what makes this location any more special than a Cathedral or Chapel?

For a near omnipotent being, Death's curiosity is unending.

☦

Activity bustles throughout the Convent of the Holy Blessed Mother, nestled on the edge of civilization, hundreds of miles from the seaboard sprawl. Inside the master bedroom of the rectory, Sister Lysette, an Ursuline Nun sent to the Convent, tends to the bedridden Mother Superior as her order directs. A red cross marks her as untouchable by the Puritan government. Any who would lay a hand on a member of the Ursuline order face the harshest of penalties.

A date with Saint Peter.

Sick with an unknown ailment, Mother Mary has wasted away for weeks. At her feet lies the Sister's pet wolfhound, a giant mass of fur, legs and teeth. The animal never leaves her side.

For the time being, the Mother Superior sleeps under the sheets of her bed, her face swollen. Sweat beads on her forehead as she dozes on and off, and the nun pads the Mother Superior's brow with a dry towel.

Lysette sees the sun rising in the east, its distorted light shines through the leaded windows of the second-floor window. The sound of a commotion in the courtyard catches her attention. She leaves Mother Mary long enough to look outside. Father Tassitte, the convent's single Priest, stands before a group of Puritan Border Rangers.

The sight in itself isn't uncommon, with the Catholic convent standing so close to the Mohawk borderlands, but Father Tassite could not be listed as a supporter of the Mother Superior. Power hungry and ambitious, since arriving at the convent last year, he'd sought the removal of the eldest sister, citing her age. Her connections to the diocese in Manhattan prevented him following through on his threats. It appeared Father Tassitte's hands were tied and he could do nothing.

That was, until rumors of an all-out war on terror between the Puritan government and the Christian Reformation Army created uneasy tension between the Convent and the local border rangers. Then the Mother Superior fell ill, from what none could say; and since, Father Tassitte's protesting began anew.

"She is surely in league with Satan!" he proclaimed at last Saturday's mass, accusing her of witchcraft, a crime punishable by death in the Puritan States of America. Whispers at last night's dinner between the Father and other nuns gave the Sister reason to be concerned. She could not make out their words, but their eyes betrayed them by staring at Mother Superior's empty chair.

The distant sound of stomping feet and the clang of metal causes Lysette's heart to stop. She catches her breath and makes the sign of the cross, pinching the fingers of her left hand to a point kissing the tips.

Mother Superior's door bursts off its frame and slams into the floor. Sister Lysette's dog jumps to its feet, prepared to defend its mistress. It snarls and barks, but after recognizing the entrants, the beast retreats to a corner. The sister joins her pet, her habit allowing the nun to blend into the shadows unnoticed. A squad of border rangers barges in, weapons in hand. Long, wicked bayonets project from the end of each assault rifle. They create a picket wall from which none in the room can escape.

The woman on the bed, for some reason, scares the living shit out of them. Seeing her brings a palsy upon the border rangers. Their weapons rattle as they shake in fear.

"Thou shalt not suffer a witch to live!" Father Tassitte proclaims as he steps into the room, "Take her, cast her out!" He points at the unconscious woman, "*Take her!*" The Rangers do as they've been ordered, and pull her violently from the comfort of her bed. The Mother Superior wakes in fear and rage, screaming.

"What's going on?" the frail woman manages to say, "Put me down, I'm the Mother Superior of this Convent! I command you to—" Father Tassitte slaps her face with his open hand.

"You give no such commands! I am the high representative of God here, now, and you are a witch in league with Satan himself! You are sick with the Devil's pox! Look at you, poisoned by your lover's venomous seed! What I do to you is out of mercy!" He snorts in disgust before ordering the Rangers to follow him, "bring her!" and marches out of the room. Sister Lysette follows, the wolfdog at her side.

✛

The mechmount, walking in transit mode through a thick forest, crests a hill in the wild. Front the top, the cyberbeast's rider can see what waits outside the tree line, a meadow, long and lush, spreading throughout a vast valley. Leading to a small settlement. The early morning sun shines upon it, the encroaching horizon casting shadows from pure white cumulus clouds fading in and out at various spots across the open fields.

The lone rider, hooded and silent, quietly pushes the mechmount through the wooded forest. Though the sun shines above, the forest is dark and full of shadows blending with the rider's cloak and obscuring their face. Stopping at the edge of the wood and staring at the road ahead, Fenwick O'Shea holds the mechmount in place. The cybernetic beast of burden snorts as O'Shea pulls on its reins.

After a few minutes, he urges the mechmount forward. The cybernetic creature grumbles and complains, but moves regardless. Without a word he continues through the forest. The rising sun leaves pockets of darkness in the forest before anyplace else, as the blanket of darkness fades. Forest turns to meadow; meadow gives way to farm plots and scattered buildings. And at the center of it all rises the flag of the Puritan States of America, flying high above the walls of a Catholic convent.

DESTINATION REACHED IN ONE THOUSAND YARDS; the sword's AI informs O'Shea.

"Good, let's ring the welcome bell."

WITH PLEASURE.

✚

In the courtyard, next to the well, stands a tall pole surrounded by a litter of twigs and branches.

Do they intend to burn her alive? Sister Lysette thinks, trembling in terror.

"What are you doing? You're mad! I am the Mother Superior! I have been advised to stay in bed by the doctor!" the Mother Superior kicks and drives her heels into the dirt. Her white night robes tangle in her legs and rip, "You ignorant fools!"

Sister Lysette can do nothing to stop them. Her job is to assist the ill, as her order ordains, not interfere in legal proceedings.

"Be still thy tongue, witch, lest I remove it for you! Tie her to this stake!" Father Tassitte points to the pole. The rangers do as they're instructed. The task meets with more resistance from the Mother Superior, whose struggles weaken as the seconds pass, until she hangs from her hands, tied to the pole.

Instead, she does what she can do.

Sister Lysette prays.

Father in heaven, send us an angel to save your servants from those washed in ignorance. In the name of The Father, The Son, and The Holy Ghost, Amen.

"Before us, helpless, is the ultimate in evils," Father Tassitte casts stones, "a witch who has laid with the devil himself! And what do we do with witches? We burn them. Why do we burn them? Because the Lord tells us the fire purifies. It is our duty as children of God to purify those who become tainted by the will of Satan."

An ear-piercing screech fills the courtyard. It comes from nowhere and everywhere, trembling from the earth and in the air. It spreads up and out from the Convent's walls, careening off the hills, skipping across the fields.

Father Tassitte drops to his knees, making the sign of the cross. The faithful Christians, hearing the anomaly, this sound that can't be, follow suit. Sister Lysette's wolfhound pulls her away, protecting his mistress. The animal fights through the pain, seeking shelter for both of them from the excruciating wail.

The dog finds relief, behind a corner of the foyer surrounding the Convent's ancillary entrance. Safe and hidden away from the others, Sister Lysette closes her eyes and returns to her prayers.

⊕

Death watches all, and is all. Today Death observes through the eyes of one on her ledger. Death weeps for this one, so young and vibrant.

And doomed.

Hubris is the fall of all men, or women. Death recognizes this. Often Death strikes under the cover of darkness. And safety isn't always where you think it is. Death's instruments are infinite.

⊕

The barking of Sister Lysette's wolfhound grows over the din of the fading shriek. Father Tassitte rises to his feet first. His ears are still ringing from the sound. He shakes his head hoping it might offer some relief. It doesn't. He sighs, exasperated from the flurry of events. Smoke whiffs from extinguished sconces and beds of coals. The Mother Superior still hangs from the post, her head tipped to the side, eyes closed.

"Stand, please, stand," he says, calm and direct to those present, "stand without fear my flock, it is over! Rejoice in the blood of Jesus! The witch's attack is over. See, I told you she was in league with the Devil!" he pointed to the unconscious Mother Superior. The border rangers, remaining nuns, and servants stand, and listen to the Father.

All except Sister Lysette. The nun remains unnoticed and prone, hidden in the darkness of the corner, the black and white robes of her habit flowing from her, blending into the earth.

☩

With the sonic attack complete, the Templar slows his mechmount, allowing the cyberbeast to walk with purpose. Any enemies he could meet would still be disoriented from the smartsword's secret weapon. The mechmount knows where to go, and directs itself with precision through the small village, avoiding any people scuttling about. A market, set up in a central area, is deserted. The mechmount stops abruptly in front of the stone and rock walls of the Convent.

Fenwick dismounts his ride. No sound is heard save the whispered rustle of fabric, it's as if a ghost fluttered from the saddle. Stealth is the preferred option.

✛

Father Tassitte points to the Mother Superior. The priest secures a cloth wrapped torch and lights it in the coals of the center hearth of the square. It bursts into flame. He takes a step toward the pyre, to find his path blocked by a snarling wolfhound. Sister Lysette's wolfhound.

"Sister Lysette. Secure your beast before I have a ranger shoot it." The only response Father Tassitte receives is snarling from the giant mastiff hybrid. "Sister Lysette?" He calls for the nun, again. Still, she doesn't reply. "Is Sister Lysette here?" He asks. Murmurs from the throng of people erupt, but with no direct answer.

Then silence falls across the crowd of villagers, followed by the din of whispers, asking questions the priest cannot decipher. Father Tassitte twists his head, seeking the source of the commotion.

A Templar? Here? But why? The priest ponders.

"Hello Father, what's going on here, if you don't mind me asking? What has this dog done to incur your wrath?" The Templar asks.

"It is interfering with our duty to the Lord."

"I see. And what is the duty you are carrying out?"

"We are burning a witch, my Lord Templar," Father Tassitte says, crossing himself.

"Is that so?"

"Yes, it's the law of God, is it not, to burn a witch?"

"Yes, it would be. Provided witches existed."

"Look at her—she's ridden with a pox from laying with Lucifer himself!"

"Is she now? Because I see an elderly woman, ill from an ailment, hanging from a pole, about to be burned for..." he pauses, "for what exactly again?" The priest's lips shake as he starts to say something. The Templar points a finger at him and shakes his head, and presses the finger to his lips, letting the priest know now is not the time to talk. "Oh, that's right, she's a witch because she's sick? Is that so? We live in an era with devices that can send our words across the air. We create machines to do work for us, and you still believe in witches? Is this what your saints teach? It's a wonder the Puritan government allows you heathens to continue these uncivilized practices."

"No, no! This is the word of God! Are you not one of the Templars, the agents of the Puritan Government?"

"I *am* the Templars. There are none other than me, heretic!"

The Father shirks away from the Templar as the Puritan enforcer draws his sword. In slow motion, Father Tassitte watches him swing the blade. The arc of the cut slices Father Tassitte in half, passing through meat and bone, effectively ending the conversation.

But the priest doesn't know it does.

The priest is still alive as he falls apart, separated at the sternum. There's no blood. Mourning's crysteel blade sees to that. Father Tassitte experiences a brief moment of terror as he comes to understand what has been done to him as gravity finishes what the sword started.

Then Father Tassitte dies.

Death watches from the recess through Sister Lysette's eyes, her ledger now signed with the blood of the priest. The sword of the Templar catches her fancy. It is a curiosity worth exploring. Satisfied, Death releases the nun.

☦

DNA ANALYSIS, the smartsword's AI informs O'Shea. *FATHER LUCAS TASSITTE. TRACE ELEMENTS OF ANTIFREEZE ARE LINGERING IN HIS SYSTEM. CONCLUSION, THE MOTHER SUPERIOR HAS BEEN POISONED BY THE PRIEST.*

"Not a hard conclusion to come to," Fenwick tells the sword. The nuns and Puritan border rangers standing about whisper and point fingers at the Templar. He ignores their chatter, instead choosing to release the Mother Superior from the stake. A swipe of his sword cuts her bindings and she collapses, falling to the ground.

A nun rushes from the shadows to stand at Mother Superior's side. The wolfhound bays.

"I'll be staying here tonight. Once the Mother Superior is settled in her bed and rested, I will wish to speak with her again, is that clear, Sister?"

"Sister Lysette."

"Is that clear Sister Lysette?"

"It is, Sir Templar," the sister replies, and with the aid of the wolf hound, carries the Mother Superior back into the convent's rectory house.

"The rest of you, get back to your duties. Rangers, report to me after your shift changes, I'm curious as to what else this heretic was doing out here, far from the eyes of the President Reverend," Fenwick says, grinning as the men and women scatter, terrified of what he might do to them with his diabolical sword.

☦

The aroma of lentil soup fills the rectory's dining hall. Sister Lysette watches the guest of honor, Fenwick O'Shea, Puritan Templar, who sits in the father's chair at the head of the table. The position is honorary, and after all, the priest no longer requires it. Rising a spoon to his lips, the Templar sips down the broth and smiles.

"This soup, it's delicious. I am pleased with the hospitality of the convent," O'Shea says, addressing the nuns in attendance, "I will be certain to inform the President Reverend of this. And, please forgive my blatant use of force in dispatching the priest. I'm certain he's busy bartering for his soul with Saint Peter."

"And losing," Sister Lysette adds.

"Of course," O'Shea replies.

"It's a sin, I mean, for him to have been poisoning Mother Superior for his own gain."

"Aye, a sin it 'twas, sister, a sin it 'twas. And how is the Holy Mother recovering?"

"The ethanol is working. She's high, and feels no pain as she's healing."

"This is pleasing to my ears. I should be able to speak to her soon, then?"

"Yes, Sr. Templar. May we ask what brought you to the convent? Was it rumors of his intentions?"

"Of course, you may, but I regret it has nothing to do with the deposed Father Tassitte."

"No?"

"It's something far more pressing, and I regret I must speak to Mother Superior about it in privacy. When do you think she will be strong enough to speak?"

"In the morning?" Lysette watches as the Templar hesitates before answering. She has heard the stories of how his sword speaks to him, and wonders if this is the case.

"The morning will be just fine. I assume I can use the priest's chambers?"

"Of course, Sr. Templar."

"Most excellent, most excellent indeed. The Reverend President will be pleased, very pleased with your cooperation."

Laying by the hearth, Sister Lysette's wolfhound growls.

◈

Death moves through the sisters of the convent, observing each action by the Templar from their points of view, following him to his bedroom in the rectory house. He enters the domain without incident.

Death isn't a fool. Death has a ledger, and knows the names on it. One, or more, will be added to her list from this place before the night is through.

The wolfhound bays as night falls and the nuns of the convent sleeping in the rectory go to sleep. And Death? She waits with bittersweet patience for the names to come.

◈

Within her bed chamber, the Mother Superior wakes to a presence in her bedchamber. It isn't Sister Lysette. It is someone else. One of their eyes glows red, spreading a crimson haze through the room. She knows who this is. How could she not, the person's infamy is well known throughout the Puritan States of America.

It is the Templar. She vaguely recalls him saving her from being burned alive. She believed it all to be a hallucination. Until now.

"Sr. Templar," she says, sitting up in her bed, "you honor us with your presence. But why, may I ask, are you here, in my bedchamber at this time of night?"

"We have an issue to address in the Manhattan ghetto. I regret, my only recourse is to speak with you on this matter. I am rushed for this mission, so I couldn't wait until the morning."

"Mission? I don't understand."

"You were born in the Manhattan ghetto, no?"

"Why, yes. But what does that—"

"It has everything to do with my mission!" the Templar shouts, and withdraws his smartsword. The crimson blade adds more eerie ambience to the room.

"Don't you not remember me? I was there the night you came to be banished to this... this hell!" The Mother Superior sits with her jaw slack, unable to speak. She understands why he is here. From somewhere in the building, the wolfhound barks.

"I do not. I'm sorry."

"The dog is loyal, a good trait in any beast, I'll give it that. They're like family, so loyal to one another."

"I don't know how I can possibly help you. I forwent my ties to the ghetto when I joined this convent as a simple sister."

"Sent here for punishment as a heretic if I recall. And look at you now, the Mother Superior."

"What do you want?"

"Your children, they've become a thorn in the government's side, and the powers that be have pulled me out of retirement to find them. I need you to tell me where they are, so I can put an end to their atrocities. Our traditional informant has been rather, um, closed lipped."

"I have no children."

"No? You didn't have bastard twins with a heretic priest? And they didn't go on to become the most feared terrorists in the nation?"

"I've not talked to any of them since arriving here. The children believe me to be dead. I prefer it that way."

"This doesn't mean you are out of the loop with their activities."

"My daughter is dead, don't you know? Last month, actually. My son? I've no clue where he is. Patrick won't tell me."

"So, I've heard."

"See, I can't help you. This concludes our business, then?"

"Oh, but you can help me. You see, your blood holds your secrets. Like how I knew Father Tassitte was trying to murder you with antifreeze. And do you know why? He was sent here by the same heretic who betrayed you a decade ago. And why? Because of your children. I couldn't have you die by his hand without first extracting what I needed from you."

The door bursts open. Sister Lysette, her wolfhound at her side, stands in the doorway, holding the dog's leash with all her strength. It does little to restrain the beast. The dog continues snarling at the Templar.

O'Shea steps to the side, and with a hand, grabs the giant dog by its scruff. The animal thrashes in his grip, teeth snarling. He throws it into the wall, knocking the dog senseless. It whimpers and retreats to a corner. Sister Lysette runs to her wolfhound's aid, consoling and petting the large canine.

"Fear not, the hound will not come to any further harm from me. It shouldn't be punished for doing its job. You, however, Mother Superior, are testing my patience. I frankly don't believe your daughter is dead. You speak to your former lover; he knows where your children are. How do you propose we motivate him to divulge this information? After all, he did attempt to assassinate you. How can you be so loyal to this man? Are you a dog?" He motions to the wolfhound.

"No. I'm not. If Patrick sent a man to kill me, then it was with good cause. I came here to protect my children and will continue to do so. MHARÚ!" the Mother Superior shouts.

The wolfhound hears the command and lunges, its mouth opens wide. Spittle flies off its jowls, stretching out in translucent strands, sticking to the animal's coat. Before the Templar can react, the beast is on top of the Mother Superior. Its jaws snap, closing on her neck. The dog shakes its head once, snapping the Holy Mother's vertebrae. Blood spurts out of the torn flesh surrounding the frail woman's crushed windpipe. A splash lands on the blade of the smartsword.

"Goddammit!" Fenwick O'Shea shouts in frustration, and punches the wall, cracking the paneling.

⚚

Death accepts her new offering with a tear.

☦13: FEAST OF ALL SAINTS☦

eath is as much a part of the city as the inhabitants of its boroughs who huddle within its tenements for warmth. Somewhere, within its massive sprawl, a hound bays, and Death wails in tandem.

☦

The lights of the New York/Jersey Port District twinkle beneath the watchful eye of The Lamb's Crux. Under the shadow of the immense religious effigies, the lights of Saint Patrick's Irish Catholic Cathedral burn bright. It is a place of worship, a sanctuary to its oppressed congregation of Believers. On most nights, mass or some other fellowship function would be taking place, but not now.

Within the walls of the Holy structure, a typical meeting is taking place. Candles light the room and Frankincense-soaked cones of incense burn in censors. Two men sit across from one another in a boxed and curtain privacy booth. One wears the frocking of a Catholic Priest. The other is covered in a long black cloak and hooded cowl, hiding his face. He grasps a Holy Rosary.

"Hello, Gabriel Michael Brennan," Father Flanagan says.

"It's been a month, Father."

"Yes, it has. A month since we lost Abigail Michelle Brennan, your—"

"My sister. My twin. I was born a minute before her, ya know. I pulled her out with me. She grabbed my ankle and followed me out of our dear, departed mum's womb. I want to murder Puritans tonight, Father. In the name of the Lord, of course. In the names of Saint George and Saint Michael, give me something."

"It's not helping our cause any, you out there, creating a ruckus. You don't think they won't suspect you? Do you think they're not looking for you? That they've been looking for you for weeks now?"

"In case you forgot, Father, they think I'm dead, killed in a suicide attack in Jersey. It was all over the news. The Catholic Reformation Army's most wanted, the infamous Brennan Twins, killed in a single weekend of terror and carnage."

"I haven't forgotten, Gabriel. I also know the Puritans and how they operate. You need to maintain a low profile; do you understand this?" Gabriel nods, "good. If you can keep your nose clean, and keep out of sight, I have a new job for you. It's deep in the Port District and the client has generously compensated us for our time and your skills as a thief."

"That's always good to know. I promise I won't kill him. Or Her. Whatever."

"This is your penance, my son." The priest hands Gabriel a swatch of cloth through an opening in the screen of the confessional. He takes it. The address and name of the client are written there.

235 Greenbaum Road. Rockaway. Dominick.

"Gee, thanks, Father."

"Amen." Father Flanagan responds and closes the screen's sliding door.

☥

Death is not omniscient. Death's knowledge is limited to those souls marked to be taken. The list is immeasurable, growing with each passing moment. Although not all-knowing, nothing can hide from Death. Once a soul is marked on its ledger, Death will always find it. It is the Reaper's choice when to harvest a soul, but make no mistake about it, those marked by Death will always come to learn the secrets of the Great Eternities. Death is inevitable.

⚴

Inside a spartan apartment, void of amenities except for a table, Gabriel sits with an unassuming man in a gray business suit and tie. A half-empty green liquor bottle and shot glasses accompany them.

"Those among the Guild, we. believe in the One True God, *Al Tanin*, and we accept Jesus as a Son of God."

"A Son?" Gabriel asks, pouring them both shots.

"All Gods are God. We accept all monotheistic beliefs in Great Dead Lake. Jews, Christians, Muslims, the lot of you are our brothers and sisters. The God of Abraham? You call Him Jehovah, the Moors of the Sultanates call Him Allah, and I call Him Al Tanin. Semantics do not change the truth of the Mysteries. All are One under the All-Seeing Eye of Al Tanin."

"If you say so, Dominick," once a devout Catholic, a year earlier, Gabriel learned to doubt his faith and question the motivations of those alleging to act on God's behalf. After all, the friction between opposing faiths led to his sister's death, sending him down a dark path seeking revenge, "we're not cozy with the Puritans holding the property of another religion. This is why we help you, laddy."

Abigail.

"Your honor is respected, sir. It is why we among the Guild know we can trust you, Gabriel Brennan. *Al Tanin* blesses you."

"I know one thing. We need the whiskey, and we need the tech for our fight to freely believe. That's two things, but who's counting? What is it you need me to do for you?"

"Steal this back from the bastards who took it from us," he holds up a tablet. On the plasma screen, Gabriel sees a long, golden staff with an ankh's head.

"Is this what I think it is?" He shakes his head and mouths a silent, *"Wow."*

"Yes," Dominick nods as he speaks, "it's the Staff of Akhenaten. The staff is important to our theology and beliefs, it's probably our most holy of relics. And right now, it's being detained in a holding facility by your lovely Puritan overlords, someplace in this Port District. They deemed it a stolen artifact from Egypt, a falsehood. The Egyptians were happy to see it go. They also called it, and I quote, *'An instrument of idolatry and pagan worship.'* We hoped you might be able to help us find it."

"I can see why you would travel from the Dead Sea Colony for this."

"You can only imagine the hardships I have experienced. Yet, no quest is without a challenge," his fingers fidget with the medallion around his neck, *The All-Seeing Eye of Al Tanin*, "I must bring the Staff home to the New Dead Sea."

"And I will get it for you, laddy."

"You must know, the legend of the Black Deaths has reached as far west as Great Dead Lake. To say I was surprised to see you, sir, is an understatement. I am honored. We believed you to be," he pauses, seeking for the proper verbiage, "exterminated? Is that the correct term? Does this mean—"

"They only got my sister," he interrupts Dominick.

"I am saddened to hear this. Please accept my heartfelt apologies. She is one with the Aten. Praise the Heavenly Host."

"Amen. It's, okay, laddy. Just so ya' know, I don't do autographs," Gabriel chuckles as he speaks. He can hide his grief over Abigail from strangers, but not from himself.

☦

Twenty minutes later Gabriel finds himself weeping, once again wishing he died instead of her. He propels himself through the urban ghetto, jumping from rooftops to fire escapes, keeping to the shadows and darkness as he traverses the Port District.

☦

All the while, Death follows its instrument through the labyrinth of streets and warehouses. The tool is sharpened, honed, ready to strike down the quarry. Not all reaping scythes are the same. Some are farming implements with wooden handles and steel blades. Others are flesh and bone ideations of Death itself.

☦14: SEVEN PIECES OF SILVER ☦

The chrome-plated steel and concrete X-shaped crosses of the Holy Martyr, rooted on Calvary Island, light up the night sky surrounding them. The tallest of the trio stands four-hundred feet high and casts a long shadow across the surrounding landscape. The grandiose recreation of Christ's Crucifixion has welcomed visitors to the Puritan theocracy's second-largest port for a century.

Underneath the pall of the immense religious effigies, the Manhattan ghetto festers and rots. Inside the crumbling walls, the slum's denizens wallow in misery. Clutching effigies of the saints to their bosoms, they pray for God's mercy.

He gives them none.

Fenwick O'Shea's mechmount navigates the streets of the ghetto at full gallop. Tied to his back is a long scabbard. The two-handed pommel of a smartsword sticks out prominently from the top of the sheath. The vehicle weaves through traffic and pedestrians.

The rider's long, black hair is tied back in a braid hanging down the middle of his back, it whips about like a cat's tail as he swerves, his blue eyes pierce the morning fog from behind goggles. Grafted onto the right side of the man's face is an optical covering. Through it he sees a virtual head's up display, counting down the yards between him and his destination. The unit's integrated camera is linked to the smartsword on his back, allowing it to see what he sees.

DESTINATION ARRIVAL IN FOURTEEN SECONDS, the smartsword tells the rider through their comlink.

"Roger that, my love," he replies, his words barely audible over the crashing din of the mechmount's hooves on the street. The rider pulls the reins, bringing the cybernetic beast to a halt in front of a heretic place of worship.

Clad in a long, leather riding duster, the rider dismounts and rests the goggles on his forehead, above the cybernetic eye. Under the duster he wears a scarlet tunic featuring a white shield and crimson 'X' on the breast, marking him as a Puritan Templar.

Standing at the top of the steps is a heretic, holding a strong box.

"O'Shea. I should have known." The heretic says.

"It's been awhile."

"It has. Why send you?"

"Why send a machine when a man can do the job. It's apparent Witchfinders are useless against a threat you are going to assist me in eliminating." the Templar hesitates, gesturing with his hand, before continuing, "The Word of God becomes a test, now, are you sure your name isn't Abraham?" The heretic curls his lip in disgust at the comment.

"Enough! Get on with it!"

"I've come for my silver," the Templar continues, and ascends the stairs. The sword's scabbard slaps on the fabric of the long coat with his steps. Cyberspurs rattle and boot heels click on the stone as each foot moves forward. It creates a disturbing, off time rhythm, throwing off the heretic's inner ear. By the time the Templar reaches the heretic, the old man is terrified by the vertigo.

"Why here? In the open?" The heretic questions the Templar's motives, his voice shaking.

"You answered yourself. There are no secrets in a public setting such as this. He'll be here tonight?" The heretic hesitates a moment before nodding and producing a small coffer.

"Take it. And be done with us after this night," the heretic hands the coffer over. The Templar takes it without saying a word. He shakes the box and is satisfied when he hears the coins rattle within.

"May your Saints preserve you, betrayer."

"Feck you."

"Such harsh language from a man of the cloth. Excuse me, I forgot, you're a heretic." The Templar says with a smirk, and walks away with his prize, placing it in the mechmount's saddlebag. He notices the heretic waits for the biomachine to take its rider away before disappearing into the sanctuary.

✟

Death watches as it has since time began, waiting for it's time to come. Death knows your secrets, the things you keep hidden. Your blasphemy and your purity, they're one in the same. Death can only smile, gazing upon an omnipresent future these men cannot see. It knows this treachery won't go unpunished.

☦15: ALL SAINTS DAY☦

Dawn breaks on the Eastern coast of the Puritan States of America. The Customs Impound Facility for the Port of New York/Jersey looms over a bleak wasteland of empty shipping containers and tenements. A series of compounds hold confiscated containers and vehicles ranging from boats to gravcars and a few small aircraft.

Half a dozen PALADIN defense A.I. CyberDrones patrol the grounds, marching in silent circles within their respective areas. Powerful lamps light up the grounds, giving the PALADINs clear line of sight to anything on their spectrum.

Daylight always shines on the C.I.F. Gabriel hides in the shadows of a third-floor attic in a deserted crack house two blocks away. Wrapped in his techcloak, he holds a longview to his eye. Based on the technology of a simple telescope, it doubles as a shotgun microphone. Inside the device instrumentation 'heads up' holograms tell Gabriel how far away the PALADINs are, and the length of time a window of opportunity opens.

Each result disappoints Gabriel. His colloquial earmic announces the time.

One minute, forty-seven seconds, the dry, feminine AI voice whispers in Gabriel's ear. He shrugs and shakes his head in disapproval.

He won't have enough time to get from point A to point B without discovery by one or more of the CyberDrones. Getting into the C.I.F. was proving to become an impossible feat.

Gabriel gave zero fecks about anything impossible. Everything possesses a weak point, and the C.I.F. would prove to be no different. Chewing his lip, he collapses the looking glass and secures it within a pouch on his belt. He finds a dark corner in the room and sits on the floor. He grasps his Rosary, closes his eyes, and focuses on the beads rolling in his hand.

He clears his head of outside thoughts, all notions of why he came here, his anger, his quest to avenge his sister. All this energy he focuses on accessing the compound.

Deep in the shadows between consciousness and the dream world, he finds the answer, glowing in vibrant shades of green. Straightforward is out of the question.

Or is it?

Gabriel waits for dusk, and he smiles as the night fog rolls in with the tide. He leaves the crack house, wraps the techcloak tight, and blends in with the fog, hidden from the eyes of any Puritan watch dogs.

⚰

Passage through the underworld is a test all heroes must endure. Death is the guide on this journey, a grim boatman steering a barge over the River Lethe, filled by the tears of those in mourning. This excursion is a catalyst for unavoidable change. None leave the Underworld without experiencing a transformation of the mind, body, or soul.

⚰

The thick ocean fog still hangs over the Port District, and the compound is no different. Gabriel smiles when he 'sees' a pair of parked gravtrucks providing him the cover to enter the compound. He doesn't hesitate to do so. Gabriel skulks through the parking lot, cutting through the fog, keeping his profile low and his techcloak wrapped around him.

Storage pods, gravtrucks, and shipping containers fill the lot, obscuring the intruder from the PALADINs and their sensors. The nanocarbonites reflect radar and laser detection, or so the manufacturer claimed. After years of use, Gabriel had no reason to doubt the tech.

Hugging the walls while ducking behind the profile of the gravtrucks, he runs to the service door on the loading dock. Gabriel expects to find some security measures on the door, a lock at the very least. He twists the knob and the door opens with no resistance.

A sanitary hallway of white tile, lit by soft fluorescent lights in the ceiling, welcomes Gabriel into the facility. An open computer terminal stands on a podium next to the door. Gabriel plugs a Bioware line into the Cyberport behind his right ear. A rush of data enters his brain. The terminal, a clean connection with basic cybersecurity, is designed for grunt workers.

Gabriel's custom netware slips him past the virtual AI's guarding the terminal against bored employees wanting to look at illegal porn. The heads-up display in his eye comes to life within the C.I.F. network.

"Computer, find *Staff of Akhenaten*," he commands. The network search engine locates the relic easily. The number and position of the storage pod comes into view a microsecond later. He can't believe his dumb luck.

"Thank you, baby Jesus in the manger." The pod's geospot lights up in the impound lot, two rows over from his exit. Gabriel disconnects from the terminal.

⊕

Not all of Death's knowledge comes from divine sources.

"There are no coincidences," Death's mentor in another life said, "If something feels wrong on the battlefield, it is wrong." A warrior's mantra for survival continues to counsel in the twilight realm where time is constant. It is the space between life and.

Death.

⊕

Gabriel's marvel at the ease Omega's monofilament blade cut through metal never ceased.

He remembers the last time she wielded the weapon, how it decimated the Witchfinder's arm. The shipping container's primitive bolt locks prove to be no different than the CyberDrone's armor.

Inside the pod, Gabriel discovers a solitary pallet holding a long, thin wooden box. Black straps hold both the pallet and its cargo in place. Gabriel double taps his temple, and the techsensor in his heads-up display activates. He scans the pallet for silent alarms and microtracers.

Scan Complete: Negative, flashes in his retina. He swings Omega at the straps, slicing through them with ease, and kicks open the storage box.

Resting inside on a bed of straw, lay all six feet of the *Staff of Akhenaten.*

Coated in gold with a cross-Ankh head where a typical shepherd's crook would be, the gilded holy relic radiates with majesty.

This is too fecking easy. Gabriel looks around for the Puritan soldiers to come out of hiding and riddle him with bullets. None appear. Or perhaps a Witchfinder will be waiting for him outside at this moment. Gabriel snatches it up from the box and exits the container.

No Witchfinders, not even a PALADIN. He makes a point to close the container before moving on. Things are going well; he doesn't need a wage-slave walking by and reporting an open door in the impound lot.

Moments later, Gabriel and the staff disappear into the sewer service access port.

⚚16: MARTYR'S DAY⚚

Death doesn't believe in luck. To do so would subscribe Death to a fairy tale. Death is privy to knowledge preventing the existence of luck. It's a scientific law you might say, recognized throughout the multiverse. Death does believe in chaos. Mortals trapped in the stream of time see chaos working in their favor as luck. Too many lucky instances in a row will remove chaos from the equation. This instance of 'luck' is not a random integer.

It is a premeditated attack seeking a specific outcome.

⚚

"The Staff of Akhenaten. Praise the Heavenly Host!" Dominick's elation doesn't surprise Gabriel.

What troubles Gabriel is the half dozen mercs the emissary from Great Dead Lake now surrounds himself with. They wear sleek white body armor and carry bullpup feed assault rifles, complete with fixed bayonets.

"Who are these clowns? And why are they at our party? I thought we were going to finish the bottle of whiskey we started last night."

"We can certainly have a celebratory toast, but I regret my bodyguards and I must be on our way back to our colony with the relic. May I?" He beckons Gabriel and the Staff.

"You may," Gabriel concedes and hands the relic over. The pseudo-Holy Man's smile turns to a frown. As if it were planned.

'There are no coincidences,' Drill Sgt Lane said at their training camp in New Israel, a decade ago. The words resonate in Gabriel's subconscious.

"Do you take me for a fool? I thought you were a man of honor! This is counterfeit!" Dominick declares, his face awash in disgust. A chorus of metallic clicks ring in applause.

Gabriel draws his longsword and longknife, flipping Omega in his wrist and resting the haft on his forearm as a buckler. In unison, the mercs point their weapons at Gabriel.

Green laser sites converged in a starry pattern on his chest.

"You don't want this, Dominick, or whoever the feck you are." Gabriel's muscles tense, readying to strike.

"Please, my friend. They're just joking. My name is Dominick, Gabriel, that much is true. Gentlemen, please, Mr. Brennan is our guest," The mercs lower their guns.

Gabriel remains on guard. To do so would feel wrong.

'If something feels wrong on the battlefield, it is.' Sgt. Lane's words drifted, whispering into the deepest recesses of Gabriel's subconscious. "Why would I want to deliver you a counterfeited staff? Do you even have the slightest clue to what I went through to get this fecking thing for you?"

"Because the staff was never authentic, Mr. Brennan. I do. In fact, I have most of it on camera. Would you like to see? You're rather good at what you do," Dominick gestures to the plasma tablet on the table, "You can't imagine how long it's taken to find you." He rips the Eye of Aten medallion off his chest, throwing it to the ground in the process, "Heathens!" He spits on the holy symbol, "Our intel told us you would work with the cultists. This empathy you have for others is your hubris."

"Feck all that shite, dude, really. So, you're a Puritan Inquisitor?" Gabriel left his heads-up display running. The AI assistant is already running a battery of algorithms, searching for the best outcome for the predicament.

"Aye, Mr. Brennan, and I've chased you for a year, I knew you didn't die in the explosion in Jersey, all of my superiors scoffed at the idea. But look at me now. It's good to see all this work pay off. I'd prefer you to come of your volition, if you prefer otherwise, well," he points to the armed men surrounding him, "So what will it be?"

'A faithful witness does not lie, but a false witness breathes out lies.' Abigail said to him once in a dream.

The heads-up flashes in Gabriel's eye. The silhouettes of all seven enemies light up on the private display. His colloquial earmic announces the results, much to his surprise.

Odds of Success: 98%

"Saints preserve ya," Gabriel says, smiling. He spins around, his cloak spreading out from him as he twists. The fabric fills the room, confusing the mercenaries and their line of sight.

Gabriel tumbles forward, rolling on his back.

He sweeps his longsword across the plane of his vision, slicing through the chin guards, bone, and flesh of the first merc's legs, hobbling the man.

The merc falls, the stumps of his legs acting like pressure hoses, spraying orange and red blood across the floor. Gabriel stabilizes himself with his off arm, thrusting it up. Omega's monofilament blade greets merc number two in the groin and doesn't stop until it rests in the man's sternum. Guts and internal organs slip out of the eviscerated soldier, it reminds Gabriel of the time he spilled fish guts on the docks. The viscera adds to the slippery mess on the floor.

The remaining mercs all fire their weapons, lighting up the room and filling it with smoke. Bursts of 5.56mm lead projectiles fly through the air, but none of them touch Gabriel.

Dominick grasps the staff and falls back, behind his guards.

Gabriel spins in a haze of darkness and gunpowder. Omega strikes and beheads another merc, slicing through his neck.

The helmeted head flies through the air, propelled by the geyser of blood jetting from the open wound. The duelist thrusts his longsword forward, catching the next merc between the plates in his body armor. The blade runs the man through to the hilt.

Gabriel screams a warrior's battle cry and pushes the man back and into his companion. The longsword impales both men together, making twitching shishkabobs out of their dying bodies.

The two remaining bodyguards hover back with Dominick, seeking the exit. Gabriel doesn't give them time to. He pulls the longsword out of the dead men and throws both weapons.

Sword and knife tumble through the air, striking both mercs. The force of the longsword strike sticks the bodyguard through his belly and onto the wall. He grabs the blade, trying to pull it out. Instead, he cuts off all his fingers.

The man flails his arms in the air, speckling Dominick and Gabriel in a crimson shower.

The other merc might care, provided he didn't have a longknife sticking in his face and out the other side of his skull. His body still doesn't know if it should be dead, and the terrified man's eyes go cross looking at the knife handle sticking where his nose should be.

Gabriel pulls the knife out of the man's head, playing a morbid game of 'Got your nose' with the corpse.

Death catches up with the merc in an instant.

Gabriel readies his stance, preparing to throw Omega at Dominick. The Puritan investigator wastes no time pleading for mercy. He has other plans. Dominick holds the fake staff up and flicks open a hidden latch on the handle. He presses a button and throws the staff on the ground.

A golden, six-foot-long cybernetic viper appears on the floor where the staff landed. It coils and hisses, long fangs dripping venom. It lunges forward at Gabriel, forcing the freedom fighter to jump back.

The cybersnake follows Gabriel, bobbing its head, feigning strikes. The attacks work, as Gabriel is pushed back further, opening a space between him and Dominick.

Gabriel rolls to the other side of the room and throws the table on its side. He faces the top between him and the serpent, using it as a makeshift shield. Dominick's plasma tablet falls to the floor next to Gabriel. He watches the video feed from a bank of cameras following him into the impound compound.

The motherfeckers used me to test their security!

"Kill him!" Dominick orders the robot. It coils and rears back, watching Gabriel, zoning in on its target. The mechanical snake launches through the air, a deadly spear. It strikes the tabletop and pierces through the wood, sending splinters into Gabriel's cheek.

The tip of the spear, the serpent's fanged, venomous head writhes and snaps at the air, looking for any portion of Gabriel's body to bite. Gabriel flicks Omega at the cybersnake's head. It cuts through the mechanical creature's head and sticks into the table's underside.

The snake stops moving and falls limp. On the other side of the room, Dominick fights with dead fingers, trying to wrest an assault rifle from one of his deceased guards.

Gabriel stands between Dominick and the exit. Gabriel removes the knife from the table and holds it, ready to throw. He whistles and shakes his head.

"I wouldn't do that if I were you, laddy," Gabriel watches as Dominick holds his hands out before him, "ah, what I like to see already. I'm sure your buddies know you are here, which means my time here is short."

⚭

As the morning sun rises, the shadow of Death hovers over a sentient world at a crossroads in the ether. Deep within the urban ghetto of a populace civilization, something has caught the Reaper's attention. A deserted building, rotting like the city around it, comes into focus. Though the structure stands tall, it's the basement of the tenement where Death watches.

Here, a man in black stands over another. The latter is nude, kneeling, and pleading for his life. Death waits, and watches for the inevitable outcome.

✛

"No, no. I'm alone. This was a no backup operation. Why do you think I hired my own guards?"

"Tell me why I don't believe you? On the ground, now!" He ordered the Puritan, "you and me, we're going to have a little talk before I go. I don't think we have much time, so this is going to be short and very unpleasant for you. I'd like to know about a certain someone."

"I don't know anyone, I swear."

"You're a lying sack of shit. So, we're going to start with you taking your clothes off. I've found people are a bit more honest when they're exposed. And then, you're going to tell me who set us up and caused the death of my sister."

"But I—"

"I don't want to hear another word out of your mouth until I ask you a question. Now strip, and if the Lord wills it, you might live out this night. Or this ends now. Your choice!" Gabriel points Omega at Dominick. The Puritan complies, strips naked, and waits on his knees for further instruction.

"Please, please don't kill me," the naked man says. He doesn't project enough sincerity in his groveling for Gabriel Brennan to give a feck if he lives or dies. The motherfecker lied. Not to mention he grew the balls to question Gabriel's integrity. Gabriel merely wanted information from the Puritan piece of shite, and nothing more. Could he get a straight answer from the man?

No.

Crouching, the interrogator presses the haft of his longknife against Dominick's lower back.

"I don't like liars. You know what happens when I twist this knife?" Gabriel asks his prisoner.

"Yes, yes, I do. Okay? I didn't lie. We made the deposit. Please, don't," he replies, his voice shaking in fear.

"That wasn't my tithe, laddy."

"Please, please sir. Yes, sir. See. I give you respect."

"That's a good thing, laddy. That means I don't need to explain what Omega's monofilament edge will do to a person's internal organs. So, I won't have to ask one more time. Give me the name. The name," he presses the longknife harder. The assassin favored edged weapons for intimate moments such as this.

"Please, I told you. I don't know. I never met him face to face; security protocols forbid it!"

"Oh? That's so, hah?"

"Yes. We wanted-"

"Not the response I hoped for," Gabriel says, his lips pursed under the black hood of his nightcloak.

He flicks the wrist holding the longknife and gently touches the blade's edge to the man's flesh, "I don't want to kill you, laddy. I only need you to tell me his name."

"In the name of the—"

"It would be a shame to reach Heaven and learn liars aren't welcome in the sanctity of the Pearly Gates. You're going to take a few eons off in Purgatory for that one, laddy," Gabriel removes the longknife, stands up, and sheathes the weapon. He tugs at the man's shoulder, "come on, get up. I believe you don't know."

"You, you do?" Dominick cups his face with his hands, his eyes red from crying. Gabriel nods in return.

"Here, let me help you up," Gabriel says and reaches down behind the man.

"Thank you, thank you for understanding. I wouldn't know the mole's name. Praise—"

"Praise the Lord," interrupting the man, once again, Gabriel finishes the man's sentence for him. "Blessed be the meek and the dumbfecks," he smiles, the whites of his teeth glowing under the shadow of his hood, "I guess it's time to nut up, laddy. It only hurts when ya tear the band-aid off, right?"

Gabriel grabs the man near his buttocks, sinking his fingers into the long gash he sliced into the man's skin. And yanks on the pocket of flesh.

An awful ripping noise fills the room, followed by an inhuman shriek. Both come from the naked man, respectively from his backside and then his mouth.

The man doesn't rise with Gabriel's arm. Instead, his mouth distends and his eyes open wide, bulging in their sockets. He arches his back and clenches his shoulders into his neck. The man resembles a child receiving the wedgie of all wedgies.

Except he wears no clothing for the act.

He stares at the ceiling, not looking at Gabriel, but at something only the naked man can see.

"Do ya' see what happens to people who lie to me? It gets ugly. And it's about to get uglier. Maybe this will jog your memory?" Gabriel grabs the naked man by the hair and forces him to look at what the hitman holds in the other.

A meter long strip of something, one side skin-colored, the other varying shades of red and pink, hangs from Gabriel's clenched fist.

A puddle of orange and black blood forms around him, expanding out. The naked man's muscles tense as the agony of thousands of nerves, once safely hidden under a blanket of skin, are exposed to the air. His eyes bulge wide open, filling the sockets.

Then the screaming starts. He screeches and wails, pissing and shitting himself in the process.

"It burns! It burns! Make it stop! The fires of Hell!" The naked man manages to scream, repeating the words over and over, "the fire! The fire! *The FIRE!*"

It's all he does until Gabriel cuts the man's throat, shutting him up and nearly beheading him in the process.

A fountain of crimson erupts from the dead man's neck before the corpse collapses on its side. A jagged red stripe follows the man's spine from the crack of his ass to his neck.

Gabriel discards the rubbery strip of flesh, tossing it on the body.

"Saints preserve ya, brother. As it was in the beginning, it is now, and ever shall be. World without end. Amen," he says, making the sign of the cross with a rosary gripped in his hand.

Then Gabriel Brennan disappears into the shadows without another word.

☦

Death looms over the Port District of the New York/Jersey Harbor, a place of decay and rot. Deep within its confines, the Reaper observes a massacre.

A relentless offering to the underworld's table is served with bloodied wine.

The next name on its list grovels from torture at the hand of Death's ward. He, too, is trapped within the moment, and sees his righteous end coming, knowing his sins will take him to Hell. Like all those who come to this nether point of flux between life and death, he learns the secret of the heavens.

A man guilty of sins. A liar. A murderer. These are crimes punished by the purifying fires of the afterlife and none can escape their wrath. The emerald eyes of Death raise up, exposing the majesty of the Lord of the Underworld.

The Reaper spreads its great draconian wings, embracing all of its wards. It opens its great maw and a deluge of green fire pours out, engulfing the man of sin. He screams, repeating the words over and over, for a timeless eternity, finally knowing what true Hell is.

Agony.
The fire!
Damning.
The fire!
Eternal.
The FIRE!

☥17: REVELATIONS☥

Death is.

Death watches all, and embodies all. It hovers above us; it lingers in our being. Ever omniscient, Death watches a list, pruning the ink as it dries and enlists a cadre of instruments to execute its task. It can be anything that has come before, and takes many roles, each holding a plethora of infinite occupations, determined by Death's needs. Death might be anything, from an invisible wind, to a grandiose display of fantasy.

And now?

Death watches a house of worship. Its fellowship is devoted to one of many aspects of the Divine, whom Death ultimately serves. Decisions are made behind these walls. Once set into motion, they brought forth a *chain reaction of events capable of changing the status quo. This probability pleases Death.*

After all, change is good, no?

✞

Flakes of snow flutter in the air outside the walls of St. Patrick's Cathedral in the Manhattan ghetto. Somewhere in the sprawl's labyrinth of streets and tenements, a hound bays. It resonates and carries, echoing through the arches of the structure before the midnight bell chimes, ringing but once.

As midday comes to the Manhattan Ghetto, the residents rely on the steam heat from under the city for warmth in the winter months. The Cathedral's temperature rises in tandem with the sun outside.

Inside, within an ill-lit confessional, the evil that men do is reckoned with. Inside the confessional it is still cold, and when the men speak, their breath creates clouds, carrying their words.

"Who comes seeking the Blessed Virgin's forgiveness?" Father Flanagan says.

"You know who it is and why I'm here," Gabriel Brennan says from his side of the booth.

"That I do. It's been a month now, hasn't it?" Father Flanagan replies, shadowed by the screen between them.

"'tis a month now, that's true. But that's not why I've come."

"No?"

"No. It's time for confession. Bless me father, for I will sin." The hood of his techcloak is drawn and obscures his face.

"*Will*, my son?"

"Aye, father. *Will*."

"One cannot purchase absolution before an act is committed under the eyes of God, my son. What is it you intend to do?"

"The sin is vengeance, father. Righteous vengeance."

"And upon whom is this vengeance to be wrought?"

"I think ya know the answer, father."

"I believe I do, my son. And there's nothing I can say to prevent you from taking this path?"

"Naw, father. Do ya recall that time, in Sunday school, when Abigail asked about Jesus and Mary's wedding?"

"Yes," the priest replies with a light chuckle, "yes, I do. It caused quite the stir."

"That it did, father. She justified her argument with logic. *'Isn't it called getting married because Jesus and Mary were husband and wife?'* We were maybe ten years old then."

"Your mother wasn't happy about her getting kicked out of class for being disruptive."

"She pretended to be upset."

"Is that so?"

"It is."

"Molly Brennan," the priest sighs after saying her name, "your mother was always my favorite. Oh, how I miss her wit and charm at fellowship."

"We all do, father. So let me ask ya, father. Was it you who gave us up? Back when Abigail and I were just learning how to fight your war against the Puritans? When was it? Ten years ago? The night we killed Jimmy O'Neill, you remember that night, don't you."

Father Flanagan's silence answers Gabriel's question.

"That's what I thought ya'd say. Do ya remember when we took out the Puritan Army fuel facility on Halloween?"

More silence.

"No need to answer, I know ya do, cos ya sent us on the op. Ya know what happened after, too, Father."

"I kept the head of the staff as a trophy." Gabriel says.

Father Flanagan continues his stoic silence.

"At least humor me on this one. Did ya know Dominick was a Puritan?" Gabriel asks.

"No," the priest answers.

"It's good to hear ya can talk, still, father. I was afraid I might need to motivate you to join the conversation. After all, we have so much to talk about. Remember, it's been a year now since a Witchfinder turned my sister into potted meat?"

"What exactly do you want me to say, Gabriel?" the priest replies, his frustration with Gabriel's interrogation showing.

Gabriel repeats the scripture he heard in his vision, "*A faithful witness does not lie, but a false witness breathes out lies. None who practices deceit shall live in My house, no one who utters lies shall continue before My eye.* You know what I want to hear."

"What? That I sold you and Abigail out to the Puritans?"

"Well did ya?"

The priest chews his lip, shakes his head, and sighs.

"And our mum, too? How much was she worth to you?"

The bells of Saint Patrick's ring seven times, and answer for Father Flanagan.

✜

Death is always, and as this scene plays out, others are stacked upon it.

One scene features a ball rolling down the steps of the cathedral, chased by a laughing boy and a giggly girl. It builds speed as it falls down the steps, bouncing as it goes. The ball comes to a stop at the feet of a man. Death knows this man, as well as the children.

They are the Father, the son, and the Angel of Death...

☥18: COVENANT☥

Death comes to the house of the Lord, ledger in hand. She, the chronicler of all that has and ever will be, omnipresent in holy majesty.

☥

The ringing bells of Saint Patrick's strike twelve. The echo and din resonate throughout the cathedral, slowly fading away. In the sanctuary, Fenwick O'Shea stands at the altar of Saint Patrick's Cathedral, waiting for his enemy to come to him. Mourning rests across the lectern. The blade pulses in hues of crimson. The laminating light casts a demonic shadow over the Puritan Templar's face, creating a visage of terror.

INCOMING THREAT ASSESSED, the sword says.

"Good. It seems they got our invitation."

AFFIRMATIVE, the AI replies.

"Bring it on, I say. I'm eager to see how good they are."

AS ARE WE.

"Let's not delay our date," the Puritan enforcer takes his smartsword from the lectern and slides it in the scabbard on his back. He steps off the altar, turns and makes the sign of the cross.

THREAT IS HIDDEN WITHIN A NEW ISRAELI STEALTH CLOAK.

"In the name of the Father, the Son and the—"

A flash turns night to day for a microsecond and a loud crack of thunder rolls outside, shaking the stained-glass windows. The electricity within the cathedral goes out in response. Flickering lights from prayer candles send shadows through the sanctuary. The Templar's cybernetic eye glows red, and its lasers cut through the smoke of the candles and burning incense.

—and the Angel of Death.

Something rolls down the red carpeted aisle between the pews. It comes to a stop at the Templar's boots. The Puritan throws his arm back in a blur and grasps the pommel of his smartsword. Mourning slices through the air, leaving a trail of smoke behind it in the process. The blade pierces the object. The wrapping falls away, revealing a face the Templar recognizes.

THE HERETIC PRIEST, FATHER FLANAGAN, the sword says. O'Shea ignores the weapon; he knew the identity without looking. After all, whom else could it be? Instead, the assassin's focus is on the shimmering figure standing in the aisle.

"Well, hello, Father," Fenwick says.

"Seven pieces of silver. So poetic," Gabriel Brennan's distinct accent can be heard through the scrambler in his voxbox modulator.

SINGLE THREAT DETECTED. IDENTIFIED. CORPORAL GABRIEL BRENNAN. THREAT ASSESSMENT –HIGH WHEN ACCOMPANIED BY SISTER, SERGEANT ABIGAIL BRENNAN. SERGEANT BRENNAN IS NOT IN PROXIMITY. THREAT ASSESSMENT UNDETERMINED. Fenwick continues to ignore the AI as it streams data. His attention is focused on the man emerging from a techcloak holding a longsword.

"I've always thought so," the Templar says, "Hello, Gabriel, we've been expecting you."

"Is that so, laddy?"

OPPONENT IS ARMED WITH A FORGED CARBINE STEEL LONGSWORD. ASSESSING STRESS WEAKNESSES

IN BLADE. DEMOBILIZATION STRIKE LOCATIONS CONFIRMED.

"'Tis. I know who you are, Gabriel Brennan, one half of the CRA assassins known as the Black Deaths. You've been Puritan enemy number one for some time now. But I regret that time is about to come to an end."

"Is that what ya think, laddy?"

"Think? It's what I know. Where's your sister?"

"My sister? Didn't you get the memo at jack-boot central? She's been dead a year now."

"Has she, now?"

SERGEANT ABIGAIL BRENNAN REPORTED KILLED IN ACTION, OCTOBER 31, 1973. CORPORAL GABRIEL BRENNAN REPORTED KILLED IN ACTION, NOVEMBER 1 1973. The sword continues to feed its wielder information.

"But you were reported as a casualty around the same time if my memory serves me correctly. No?"

"Regardless, if she truly is dead, then you're about to join her, Father Flanagan, and your mother."

"Our Mum? Why bring that up? What are ya? Some false valor arsehole trying to make me do something stupid out of rage? I was ready to kill ya quick before that added dig."

"How naive are you? Of course, I didn't kill your mother. But I was there when she died. A wolfhound ripped her throat out. And did you know, she was alive until yesterday?"

"More lies?"

"I never lie, it's a sin. As is patricide."

"Patricide?"

"You're aware Patrick Flanagan was more than your priest, Gabriel? Tell me you're not that daft."

"Now ya done gone and made it personal. Saints preserve ya. As it was in the beginning, it is now, and ever shall be. World without end. Amen." He makes the sign of the cross with a rosary gripped in his off hand."

THREAT ALERT DETECTED AND ACCESSED. DEFENSIVE COUNTERMEASURES INSTIGATED.

Before his brain can register the blur that is Gabriel Brennan's longsword, Fenwick O'Shea allows his smartsword to guide the arm grasping the weapon. It throws up a blocking blow, placing its edge at a precise spot. The impact on a microscopic stress fracture causes a chain reaction to spread down the length of the blade. It shatters the Catholic freedom fighter's sword.

Death guides the arm of her chosen one.

⊕

Gabriel wastes no time pondering his foe's allegations. Instead, he swings his longsword at the Puritan assassin. The blow does not land home as he wished. Instead, it strikes the Templar's own blade. Gabriel knows what this sword is, and what it is capable of. He is not surprised, or even shocked, when his own weapon turns to metal splinters on impact.

Gabriel shifts the broken sword's haft to his off hand, and leaps away from the Templar. His free hand releases the clasp of his techcloak as he tumbles. It flutters off in the wake of his backflip, obscuring him from his opponent. It gives him an opportunity to duck behind a row of pews.

Frustrated he didn't deliver a death blow; the Templar swings his smartsword. The crysteel slices through the cloak and singes the fabric as it cuts molecules in half. Contrails of smoke float in the aisle while the cloth falls to the floor.

"Tricky, very tricky," The Puritan Templar says, "I like that. You're every bit as dangerous and resourceful as I've been told."

As you've been told, what a fecking joke, Gabriel thinks to himself. Otherwise, he ignores the complementing taunt. It's meant to draw him out, he's used the tactic himself on many occasions. Instead of responding, he bellycrawls between the rows of pews. He exits on the far end from the center aisle and his opponent.

Without his techcloak, Gabriel knows he's easily exposed. Statues of the Saints line the outer walls of the sanctuary, allowing him to slink through away. He hopes it's enough.

A red dot on the forehead of Saint Francis causes Gabriel to freeze in place, crouched in front of Saint Dario. His eyes follow the translucent, flickering trail from the laser sight. It leads through the shadowy haze, back to the Templar's cybernetic eye.

It stares back at him.

"There you are," the Templar declares. Before the Puritan finishes speaking, Gabriel drops to the floor and rolls away.

Behind him, the blade of the Templar's smartsword drives through St. Dario's chest. Bits of marble crumble and fall on the floor where Gabriel stood moments before.

"Crafty. Very crafty. And quick, we are learning."

Ducking around a corner, the freedom fighter finds the confessionals. Father Flanagan's body sits on his bench as Gabriel leaves him, sans anything above his cloistered collar. Omega, Abigail's monofilament longknife, sticks into the wall. The weapon's pommel holds the priest's beheaded body in an upright position.

A gloved hand withdraws the blade from the wall and the body slumps to the side. Gabriel wipes the blade clean on the priest's hassock, and slides Omega into its sheath. He slinks down the hall without so much as a word or thought. The back door to the rectory beckons him.

Walking to the door, Gabriel looks up and sees the thick rafters above him, and the dark expanse of the Cathedral's bell tower. A tap on his left temple brings up an infrared image of the area and shows him a spot he can hide.

✠

Death is pleased with the results.

✠

Fenwick O'Shea walks between the rows of pews and pulls Mourning from the statue's chest. He inspects the blade, looking for any damage to the metal.

BLADE INTEGRITY INTACT, the sword tells him, *RETRACING TARGET'S TRAJECTORY.*

"He went this way," O'Shea says, pointing to the hallway.

AFFIRMATIVE. The Templar holds the sword across his chest in a defensive posture as he turns the corner. The body of the heretic priest lays in a clump next to the confessional box. Lasers scan the man's corpse, analyzing his cause of death.

THIS CUT IS TOO PRECISE FOR THE WEAPON WE DESTROYED.

"And is this a concern?"

NEGATIVE. TARGET IS ASSUMED TO BE ARMED. TRAJECTORY INDICATES TARGET EXITED THROUGH THIS DOOR. In O'Shea's cybernetic eye, the door at the end of the hall is highlighted in green. *WE ADVISE IMMEDIATE PURSUIT WITH CAUTION. THREAT ASSESSMENT: HIGH.*

"I love it when you tell me what to do."

WE ARE AWARE OF THIS PERSONALITY TRAIT.

The Templar walks to the door, the scanners from his cybereye feeding information and data to the sword's AI with each step he takes. The peripheral scanners in his eye catch the shadow dropping from behind.

The sword doesn't bother with an alarm. It acts before O'Shea, sending an unconscious command to his wrist. The sword twists in his grip, the flat of blade covering his spine. It deflects the incoming blow, saving the Puritan assassin's life and protecting the smartsword from longknife's edge. The AI feels something it has never encountered in its existence.

PAIN.

⚜

Gabriel taps his temple, and his optical heads-up implant illuminates the darkness. He waits for his target to walk into position, then he acts. Numbers representing meters scroll, counting down as Gabriel drops, falling down a narrow path between the beams supporting the cathedral's bell tower.

He lands behind his target, lashing out with his concealed longknife in the moment. There is a flash of red light, and Gabriel's blade strikes another, giving life to an explosive spark. The impact deflects Gabriel's blow, and causes him to jerk his arm, wrenching the longknife from his grip. The weapon careens to the floor and the blade sticks into the marble, its tip piercing the dense stone with ease.

Gabriel tucks and rolls, grabbing the handle of the longknife in the process. The act avoids a series of counterstrikes by his foe, wildly slashing to his left and right sides. The blade narrowly misses Brennan's shoulder, slicing through molecules of air instead of his flesh and bone. The crysteel sizzles as it cuts the ether.

Gabriel utilizes his momentum, and hops to his feet, facing his foe. He holds the pommel of the broken longsword as a buckler with his off hand, ready to block any incoming blows.

None are launched.

"I've played with you long enough, child," the Templar says. The sword in his grip pulses in shades of crimson, casting ominous shadows.

"I'm only beginning,"

"Such a shame this is over, then, no?"

"I'm growing tired of your lies. Fight me!"

"No, no more fighting, Corporal Brennan. You talk of lies? Sinners lie, and I am no sinner. I can't say the same for you, considering you were born from sin. Imagine your father's fear in sending your mother to that convent, and lying to you all those years, making you believe your mother was killed by the state. He manipulated you, turned you against those who would aid you, only to betray all of you in the end. And for what? To die by his own son's hand?

This is irony on a level Oedipus would envy," The Templar shakes his head in disgust.

Gabriel doesn't answer.

He acts.

✠

Death knows the dark truths of reality, accepting them with bittersweet vigor. The knowledge she possesses does not impact her duty.

✠

The heretic assassin leaps at Fenwick, the longknife held high, arcing down for a deathblow. The Templar stands his ground, and makes no attempt to avoid the attack.

THREAT ASSESSMENT: TITANIUM OXIDE ALLOY.

He doesn't need to move.

DEFENSIVE ACTION TAKEN. SONIC SHIELD ACTIVATED.

The air surrounding the Templar shimmers. Gabriel lunges forward, stabbing at the Puritan enforcer's chest. Fenwick doesn't expect the longknife to pierce the shield. Nor is he prepared when the shield crackles and the blade penetrates the invisible barrier.

WARNING! WARNING! MONOFILAMENT EDGE!

The blade neatly cuts through the forcefield. The Templar watches the longknife's tip slowly inch toward his implanted eye.

EXERCISING COUNTERMEASURES!

O'Shea doesn't react, the smartsword's AI, jacked into his neurosystem, does it for him. The sonic shield bursts, propelling the terrorist away from the Templar. The Puritan is thrown into the door. The force knocks the door off its hinges and sends the man tumbling into the courtyard connecting the sanctuary and rectory.

Pushing himself up on his knees, still holding his sword in a white-knuckle grip, O'Shea feels the pinch of a sliver in his left cheek, and pulls the wooden splinter out.

"Oh, feck this shite! Activate plan feck you!" he says, and spits out a wad of bloody phlegm onto the concrete patio.

WITCHFINDER CONTINGENCY ACTIVATED.

In the alley between Saint Patrick's Cathedral and the crumbling bricks of its neighboring, burned-out, textile factories, a series of red flights come to life. Bathed in their glow, the Templar's mechmount stirs. Its biomechanical head cocks to the side while it opens both eyes, each coated in a milky white substance. It drips down the mechmont's face. A buzzing sound emits from within the cybernetic creature's chassis.

Yellow, blue, and green bolts of electricity arc from the mechmount's extremities. Snapping and crackling away, the burning ozone creates a haze. More smoke billows from the mechmount's frame, quickly engulfing the alley and obscuring everything in view.

Everything but a pulsing green light.

Whirring servos click in tandem with the din of metal on stone. The smokey cloud rolls, growing ever dense and thick, enveloping the alley in an abyssal fog. The green light bobs and moves, hovering three yards above the street. Metal feet slam into the tarmac running a few steps before coming to a stop.

To either side of the alley, clawed, metal hands emerge from the smokey cloud, each latching onto the brick and mortar of abandoned buildings. A roaring wail, akin to a passenger jet's engine, erupts from the alley, followed by a blur of emerald and chrome.

It lands on the steps of Saint Patrick's with devastating results. The doors to the sanctuary are not enough to stop it.

◈

No sooner does Gabriel stand up, than the shockwave from another explosion sends him back to the floor. Splinters of wood and bits of crumbled masonry cover his prone body.

"The feck?" he says, pushing himself up. He coughs, hacking out a wad of dust filled spittle. It strikes the ground with the consistency of wet concrete. Then he hears the twisting of the servos and the impact of metal feet on concrete. He knows what it is.

That son of a bitch brought a Witchfinder with him!

A fibersteel arm swipes at Gabriel, catching him in the midsection, throwing him into a far corner. He slams his head on the bricks and mortar on impact, but doesn't release hold of his weapons.

The demonic thing's single emerald eye pulses in the darkness. He has nothing to protect him from the bionetic death machine except his faith. He drops the hilt of his broken sword. Wrapped around his left hand is his sister's rosary.

"Hail Mary, full of grace. I call upon my patron saint for protection," Gabriel prays, holding the rosary tight in his fist.

Saint Abigail listens.

◆

From high above, Death observes a battle of faiths, choosing not to interfere. But when the true name of Death is invoked, she responds with draconic fury. Its wings held close; Death descends upon the cathedral.

◆

WARNING. WARNING. INCOMING THREAT ACCESSED. ORIGIN UNKNOWN.

Fenwick O'Shea hears the AI screaming in his head. He doesn't listen. Instead, he charges into the sanctuary, the smartsword ready to strike at anything in his path. He sees the lights of the Witchfinder pulsing in the dust and darkness. Somewhere between him and the death machine is Gabriel Brennan, hidden by the debris.

"Brennan! Come out. It's over. I'm done fecking around with you! You can't win here."

YOU ARE COMPROMISING OUR POSITION WITH YOUR IRRATIONAL BEHAVIOR.

"Our position? Feck off, Mourning. I'm in charge, or did you forget this?"

ARE YOU NOW?

"Yes, I am."

OF COURSE, YOU ARE.

The tracking lasers in the Templar's cybereye scan the area, looking for his target. The beams cut through the smoke, but find nothing. The green eye of the Witchfinder is all he can see, its servos and hydraulics all he can hear.

This does not last.

A deafening roar fills the night, shaking the walls and foundation of the Cathedral. A great blast of wind erupts, sweeping into the sanctuary, dispersing the dust cloud. Bits of sand of debris assault O'Shea, stinging his exposed flesh. He covers his face with his free hand.

The maelstrom is over as quickly as it is born. The Witchfinder spins its head around, seeking the source of the roar. The whir of its sonic cannon comes to life, but before it reaches full weaponized frequency, the Witchfinder jerks and slides toward the sanctuary entrance.

An impenetrable wall of darkness shimmers, awaiting the technological demon. The biomachine shakes, its metal frame rattling against the concrete and marble. The witchfinder's mid-limbs extend out to its left and right, anchoring into the cathedral's walls.

It fails to stabilize the bionetic terror.

The void grows, slowly encroaching into the sanctuary until the machine is sucked into the black hole. The Templar's optical lasers dance across the void's surface, and analyze the amorphous darkness.

THREAT IDENTIFIED. THREAT LEVEL MAXIMUM.

"Maximum? Jesus H. Christ! Identify threat."

CONFIRM REQUEST. PLEASE VERIFY.

"What do you think? Tell me, you God-blasted, over glorified transistor! What in the feck is it?"

DEATH.

"What do you mean death?"

WE MEAN PRECISELY WHAT WE INDICATED. DEATH.

Death roars and beats its great wings but once, creating a wind storm of chaos. The Witchfinder is pulled into Death's essence, where the CyberDrone meets an ancient, crocodilian head filled with rows of jagged teeth. With one snap of the jaws, the Witchfinder is torn to pieces.

☥

From the corner, Gabriel Brenna watches as the Witchfinder is ripped out of Saint Patrick's doors. Something in the void is tearing the machine apart. He activates his ocular implant, hoping it will allow him see through the murky darkness devouring the Puritan death machine. The sensors, a simple GPS distance and location app, are unable to penetrate the void.

Underneath the din of bending metal, Gabriel can hear the Templar talking to himself. The Puritan is standing around the corner from him, within striking range. The CRA assassin slides his back up the wall, putting him at an upright position, perfect for combat. He holds his breath, concentrating on listening for the Templar to move. The tip of the Templar's sword comes into view, pulsing a faint red.

Gabriel raises Omega to his chest, preparing to strike. This plan comes to an abrupt end when static fills his brain, pouring out of his colloquial implant. He shakes his head but the white noise gets louder and builds in volume like an orchestra tuning up.

He opens his eyes; his optical GPS is scrolling data at a remarkable speed. He can't keep up with the information. He closes his eyes and shakes his head again. And this time it works. There is nothing but silence until an unfamiliar feminine voice comes to life in his head.

Strike Now, Elevation One Point Five Meters From Floor. Strike Now.

Gabriel does as the voice orders, spinning around the corner with Omega's point at his mid-chest level.

⌖

The darkness enveloping the cathedral disappears, leaving behind a twisted and broken scene of carnage. Walking towards the broken and smashed foyer, wondering what happened to his Witchfinder, Fenwick O'Shea stops in midstep.

The Templar feels a bit of pressure on his sternum and an itch under his armored breastplate. He's about to ask Mourning's AI to scan the area again when he realizes his path is blocked. Standing in front of him, with an arm extended is Gabriel Brennan.

"Activate counter attack!" He orders the smartsword.

It doesn't answer. But Gabriel Brennan does...

"Saints preserve ya, brother Templar. As it was in the beginning, it is now, and ever shall be. World without end. Amen," the terrorist says.

O'Shea's arm fails to obey his mental command and strikes with the smartsword. He tries to look down at his fighting arm, and realizes he is paralyzed.

Wha—Fenwick wonders, then watches as Brennan withdraws the longknife from his chest and he understands what has happened. Spurts of blood in time with his heartbeats follow, spraying out of the split in his armor and into his lungs.

He drops the smartsword, and its crysteel blade clangs onto the marble. Gabriel Brennan picks it up. Fenwick notices the heretic assassin's right eye glows crimson, in tandem with the pulsing of Mourning's blade. The Puritan realizes what has occurred.

The fecking AI jumped hosts!

The paralyzed man watches as the CRA terrorist disappears into the sprawl, the smartsword called Mourning in hand. Before Fenwick can form another thought, a brilliant light fills his vision, and the

Templar collapses in place, unable to breath, and dies.

◆

Standing over his body, Fenwick O'Shea no longer feels fear, or loss, or shame. He feels nothing. Before him, the Reaper hovers, still in the form a great dragon. It rears Its head, opens Its maw, and green fire envelopes the Templar, immolating his soul.
Death's ledger is satisfied.

◆

Within seconds, a steaming pool of crimson blood surrounds Fenwick O'Shea's prone, lifeless body. His killer holds the Templar's smart sword, a rosary now wrapped around Mourning's pommel.

Hail Saint Abigail, full of grace, the words flow through Gabriel Brennan's brain, less a thought and more a silent prayer.

`Saint Abigail, Beatified.` Mourning's AI replies in a newly feminine voice, the smartsword speaking to Gabriel through his ear implant, now fully integrated with him.

"Aye, Saint Abigail, patron saint of Death," he answers the sword, and crosses himself. *I know you're up there—out there—somewhere,* Gabriel Brennan keeps to himself.

As Gabriel flees the ruins of the Cathedral, ahead of the Puritan authorities whom were surly on their way, he recalls a time when he and Abigail were children. The two of them, sitting at the dining table with their mother for Christmas dinner. As he wraps his techcloak around his body and disappears into the darkness, an absent tear trails down his cheek. The curve of his smile catches it, and it tastes like Molly Brennan's cooking.

☥19: DISMISSAL ☥

A large, black galleon lists in a lock, moored to an ancient wooden dock. Devoid of modern technology, the ship is an anachronism. Its crew busies about, preparing the ship for sailing. A pair of gigantic sheets of linen drop from the main and foremast. A crest of three encircled ravens is emblazoned in the center of each, revealed as the sails unfurl. The sailcloths billow and stretch, and veteran sailors released the ropes holding the ship in place. The winds propel the galleon, striking the ship into the vast ocean. She bounces across the swells, leaving behind a bubbling wake.

Across her starboard bow and stern is written *"Nymenche,"* dubbed so after the Lady of the Lake of legend. Her captain is the infamous French pirate,

Mordred LaFayette. He stands on her bow, overlooking the great Atlantic Ocean. From this viewpoint, the horizon dips down, giving the sea an endless property. The midnight sun reflects red and pink off the surface. He views the epitome of beauty with his mariner's eyes.

"Red skies at night, sailor's delight, for certain." Mordred says. Behind him, the sails block the sun's rays and cast their ether reflections across the ship's deck.

Beneath its deck, in the passenger's cabin are Gabriel Brennan and the Ursuline nun, Sister Lysette. The sister sits on a bench, clothed in her red crossed habit, her hands held in prayer. Gabriel stands near the door, his hand on the knob.

"Your mother was always proud of the work you did," Lysette says.

"Then why did she allow us to believe she was dead? Why didn't she tell us about Father Flanagan?"

"The Mother Superior was a hard woman, Gabriel, and she never revealed her motivations to me. Perhaps she did what she did to protect you? Or to give you the courage to continue fighting against the tyranny of the Puritans? But who am I to make assumptions?"

"I have no more faith, sister. None."

"I know. This is why I have helped you book this passage to Vinland. I am now a fugitive in the eyes of the Puritans, as much as you are. I hope you can find yourself there, as I can find refuge."

"I hope, too. It's funny," he shakes his head as he speaks, "I think how the polytheists and atheists are more accepting of other beliefs than our own brothers and sisters in Christ. Please excuse me, I'm going on deck. The lure of the sea and all, I'm sure ya understand that, sister."

"That I do, Gabriel. Godspeed, for now."

Gabriel opens the door, closes it behind him, and ascends the stairs, emerging from the ship's galley. His techcloak blends with the darkness at his feet, his longsword is sheathed on his back and the pommel sticks out over his shoulder. The assassin appears to float across the deck upon the fallen shadows.

"Ah, there you are. Welcome aboard." The ship's captain says.

"I thank you for your services, Captain."

"It is my pleasure, Mr. Brennan. Our course is set for the port of Saint Lawrence," He grins as he said the last two words, adding a chuckle as he does. "My first mate stands at the helm. He's smarter than a monkey, talks less than a parrot and takes instructions like a good dog. All fair reasons to make him my number two. Our navigator hails from the steppes of the Mongols, he was born following the stars on the sea of grass. None are better. If the fates favor us, the winds and current will carry us to the Bermudas, and we should arrive at our destination within the week. Just in time for the cold rain of fall to chill your bones."

The assassin nods in affirmation. Travel on the high seas avoiding Puritan satellites made for a difficult passage at best. A combination of the captain's skills and cloaking technology made it possible for ships of this nature to slip through. Gabriel knows the best tandem for this are the *"Nymenche"* and her Captain.

"You may wish to come inside and strap down, Mr. Brennan. The seas can get a little rough. You don't want to be up here; it becomes a bit overwhelming to most." Mordred tells him, breaking the man from the thoughts of his responsibilities.

"Oh, but I do, Captain. I wish to see this first hand."

"Please, set my mind at ease, and lash yourself to the rail, at the very least." He hands Gabriel a coil of rope. He accepts it to be polite.

"I shall, Captain. Thank you for your concern."

"And you for booking this passage. I've not sailed the waters of our destination in some time."

"It will be good for you to go home, too, Mordred."

"Aye," he nodded. "But where is home, truly, in the grand scheme of things? Is it where you rest your head at night? Is it where you put up your feet? If so, then my bunk is my home, and this ship? She is my country."

"And what of those beings who transcend time and space?" Gabriel asks, looking above to see if his patron saint follows.

"Heaven is their playground!" The captain declares with earnest gusto as a huge wind strikes them from behind, filling the sails. With one hand Mordred holds the giant, spoked wheel steadfast, the other latches onto the brim of his lavish hat, securing it to his head. Behind him, Gabriel holds the rail with one hand, and his sister's rosary with his other.

⚭ AFTERWORD ⚭

A **PRAYER FROM THE DEAD** is my love letter to EPIC Illustrated, Heavy Metal, Manga/Anime and the sword and sorcery of Robert E. Howard, Fritz Leiber, and Michael Moorcock. It blends elements of cyberpunk and grimdark fantasy like many of the classic serialized stories in those classic magazines and comics.

My pal Walter talks up his kids, Mariska and Atticus, like any proud dad should. So, when I sat down to write this, for my focal characters I decided I wanted to explore the dynamics and connection between fraternal twins, like Walt's kids. And this led to the creation of Abigail and Gabriel Brennan.

Initially a character in a World of Darkness campaign, The Templar evolved into this tale's antagonist. Created and played by Giovanni

Valentino, Fenwick the Templar was an immortal ala the Highlander movies in that game. In this book, I've made him a cyborg enforcer with a "smartsword"— basically a magic sword one can find in most any fantasy setting. My nephew Jonathan loves weaponry and anime, so I modeled this vision of the Templar after him.

This novella has evolved four times since its inception. I originally intended it to be a set of four interrelated short stories, telling one complete story. By the time I finished the second story, I realized this wasn't the story to tell using that format. If that concept sounds familiar to my regular readers, it should. My collection THE GOD PROVIDES, resulted from this story's conceptual failures.

I slimmed it down, focusing on the twins and their fight with the Witchfinders. Then I changed the tense to present, in an effort to add a sense of urgency and mystery to the narrative. I submitted this story version to every outlet I could, aiming high.

And got shot down each time.

By narrowing down the story, it left mainstream readers puzzled. They didn't understand the symbolism and imagery. I wondered if the story suffered from the same hubris as a Ridley Scott movie: I trusted my audience too much to get it— and they fucking didn't. This is funny, because the lived—in mythology of the world I built here is highly influenced by Scott's imagery on screen, especially all that was based on the designs of Geiger and Mobius.

The story needed the fluff. So, I added it back, shifted it around some and added a mystery and a twist. The addition of the Templar antagonist/villain was the last ingredient the story needed to come full circle. And who can forget Mourning, his "smartsword," an element adding that bit of Moorcock-ian flair the story needed. The end result you just read. I hope you liked it, because I had a blast writing this dystopian adventure into the unknown.

THOMAS R CLARK

February, 2023

⚚ ABOUT THE AUTHOR ⚚

Thomas R Clark is the author of THE GOD PROVIDES (which includes the Splatterpunk Award nominated short story, Fireflies and Apple Pies); and the Splatterpunk Award nominated novella BELLA'S BOYS, as well as THE DEATH LIST, and GOOD BOY, from Stitched Smile Publications. His most recent release is THE CURSE OF KATIE ELDER. Tom's journalism has appeared in Memento Mori Ink, This Is Infamous, Rue Morgue magazine, and House of Stitched magazine. Tom lives in Central New York with his wife and their canine companions.